SMALL
FRY

Books by David Baddiel

ANIMALCOLM

BIRTHDAY BOY

(THE BOY WHO GOT) ACCIDENTALLY FAMOUS

FUTURE FRIEND

HEAD KID

THE PARENT AGENCY

THE PERSON CONTROLLER

THE TAYLOR TURBOCHASER

VIRTUALLY CHRISTMAS

ONLY CHILDREN

SMALL FRY

DAVID BADDIEL

SMALL FRY

ILLUSTRATED BY
CORY LOFTIS

HC
CB
HARPERCOLLINS
CHILDREN'S BOOKS

First published in the United Kingdom by
HarperCollins *Children's Books* in 2024
HarperCollins *Children's Book*s is a division of
HarperCollins*Publishers* Ltd
1 London Bridge Street
London SE1 9GF

www.harpercollins.co.uk

HarperCollins*Publishers*
Macken House, 39/40 Mayor Street Upper
Dublin 1, D01 C9W8, Ireland

1

HB ISBN 978–0–00–862195–7
SPECIAL EDITION ISBN 978–0–00–873121–2
TPB ISBN 978–0–00–862196–4
PB ISBN 978–0–00–862198–8

Typeset in ITC Novarese Book 12pt/23pt
Printed and bound in the UK using 100% renewable electricity at CPI Group (UK) Ltd

CHAPTER 1

"Burger, please, mate."

"With onions?"

"What?"

"WITH ONIONS?"

"Oh, yeah."

"Is there ketchup, mate?"

"It's by the side of the van . . ."

"Mayonnaise?"

"Yes, that too."

"Two dogs, Lenny . . ."

"Two hot dogs? Hang on – I'm just doing this bloke's burger."

"Well, get on with it. The match is starting in a minute . . ."

It was the same every Saturday. The same words, more or less, said by the same, more or less, people, queuing up outside the same burger van. They might have had different faces, but they were all bound by one thing, which is that they were all fans of Bracket Wood FC, one of the least exciting football clubs in the Southern and District Local Semi-Pro League Division Three. Which, as you can probably tell from its name, was itself not the most exciting league in the game.

But one of the people saying those words wasn't more or less the same. The man saying "With onions?" and "It's by the side of the van" and "Hang on – I'm just doing this other bloke's burger" was exactly the same.

Because he was Lenny Burns, who owned the burger van. This was made apparent by the sign painted on the top of it: **Lenny's Burgers**. I'll let you in on something about Lenny Burns: he didn't like to spend too much time thinking about things. Like, for example, what he should call his burger van.

"Come on, Lenny, mate!" repeated the hot-dog-requiring person, who was a woman. Her name was Edith, and she had been coming to see every Bracket Wood FC game since 1953. She'd never missed one, and that included a period when no one was allowed into the ground for an entire season because of an illness everyone was worried about. Edith had dealt with that by renting a flat in a tower block that overlooked The Bracket[1] and watching those games through binoculars.

It was quite hard to see what Edith looked like, or indeed hear what she was saying, as she wore a lot of scarves. These were, of course, Bracket Wood

1 The name of the Bracket Wood FC stadium. "Stadium" is quite a strong word for it – it was more . . . four corrugated iron shacks around a muddy rectangle of grass.

FC ones. Bracket Wood FC's colours were blue, as they wore blue shirts and blue shorts, which made the team when they came out of the tunnel look like a more famous football team. But that illusion was soon dispelled when the match started. In fact, sometimes during the warm-up.

Anyway, Edith wore at least five of these scarves. Plus a bobble hat, which she pulled down quite far over her face, even in summer. Which meant that the most visible part of her was her mouth, which at the moment was both speaking and salivating.[2]

"I'm always in me seat before kick-off! Always!" the mouth said.

2 I'm sorry. I know this is quite a long word that some readers may not know. It means, basically, that she was dribbling a bit – that dribble being brought on by hunger and the hot-dog smell. I'm also sorry if you've come to this footnote and now feel sick.

"Well, maybe just don't have the hot dogs this time?" said Lenny. He was sweating while trying to flip one of the many burgers on the grill in front of him. He wore a T-shirt and an apron that at one time had been white but now was mainly the colour of burger grease. Across that was written **Lenny's Burgers**. And also the words: "If You Want A Burger, Get It Here." That was the slogan of Lenny's van. As I say, he was a man who didn't like to spend too long thinking about anything. The slogan had once been painted on the overhang[3] as well, but that bit had fallen off a long time ago.

"I always have two dogs as well! That's one of me superstitions!"

"Your superstitions, Edith?" said Lenny, re-flipping the burger and piling on some onions. "So . . . that'll be things you do every week because you believe they somehow help the team to win, right?"

"Yes!" she said. "Every week!"

"OK. So given that Bracket Wood haven't won

3 I think that is what you call it. It's basically the bit of a burger van that opens up to reveal the cooking area, and also serves as a shelter to the people waiting to eat. To be clear, I don't own a burger van and have never worked in a burger van, so some of the technical language might be beyond me.

anything . . . hang on – let me check my notes . . ." Lenny didn't have any notes, but he pretended to be looking down at some form of record book. "Oh, that's right . . . EVER – maybe the superstitions don't work as well as all that?"

Edith frowned, as if she couldn't compute what Lenny was saying. Then she looked, for a second, quite upset.

"So . . . you're saying . . . I shouldn't have me dogs?" she said weakly.

"Dad," said a voice from beneath the grill. "I'll do it."

CHAPTER 2

"Who said that?" said the burger-wanting man.

"Small Fry!" said Lenny, as he handed over the actual burger to the man. It was a dry-looking meat patty stuffed into an even-drier-looking bun, packed to the brim with onions. With his other hand, he reached over and put a stool in front of the grill.

Stepping on to it – and therefore into vision for Edith, the (now) burger-munching man and the queue of hungry people behind them – was a boy of about eleven. In contrast to Lenny, who as we know was not dressed in a particularly pristine way, the boy was wearing a set of perfect chef whites. All in white, that is, with a white apron and a white chef's hat.

"Hello, Benny . . ." said Edith.

"Hello, Edith!" said Benny. In his hand was a spatula. He placed it on top of two very long sausages on the grill and pressed. They sizzled. In his other hand, he held a stopwatch.

"How's the job as assistant chef going?" asked Edith.

"Brilliantly, thanks!" He spread open two long rolls and placed them bread side down[4] on the grill to toast.

"This is my son, Benny!" said Lenny. "I call him Small Fry! Because he's small and he fries!"

"Yes," said Edith. "I know all that. You tell me every week."

"Benny does great work for me!" said Lenny. "I don't know what I'd do without him."

"Well, I for one am glad you're doing me dogs, Benny!" said Edith, with a small hint of getting one back on Lenny for making fun of her superstitions.

4 I also don't actually know much about cooking despite writing a novel about it. By bread side down, I mean the white bit of the hot-dog roll. Does this have a name? Who knows. Not me. You know, the inside.

"You're the best cook in this van anyway!"

Lenny jokingly waved his spatula at her, like it was a light sabre[5]. "Careful, Edith. I'll tell him to undercook them . . ."

"I won't listen anyway, Dad!" said Benny. "I always do hot dogs for seven minutes and forty-three seconds, which is the perfect time for them to be firm but not dry!"

"Seven minutes and forty-three seconds!" squawked Edith. "But the match starts in five!"

"Don't worry, Edith," said Benny, checking his stopwatch. "These two have already been on the grill for six and a half minutes, so . . ." He gave the sausages a final hefty press, while keeping one eye on the watch. "OK!" Deftly, he lifted both of them with the spatula. With his other hand, he picked up the rolls, catching the sausages as they slid inside.

"Onions?" he said.

5 A light sabre is a weapon from *Star Wars*. I have no idea if any children reading this know what *Star Wars* is any more. If you don't, it's a kind of sword that lights up. The spatula didn't light up, so this may have been a stupid thing to compare it to.

"Of course!" replied Edith. "I always have onions with me dogs!"

Benny's spatula dug into the third section of the grill, which had the onions cooking on it. He lifted a large dollop and carefully sprinkled them on to each hot dog.

"There you go!" he said, handing them over. "Ketchup and mayo . . ."

"At the side of the van! I know!" said Edith, moving off quickly. "Thanks, Benny!"

"I'd recommend the spicy relish too. I got my dad to buy that after I tried it last week!"

"She's gone, Benny," said Lenny.

"Burger, please, mate," said a new voice.

"Shall I do that as well, Dad?"

"Small Fry, I do the burgers – you know that."

"But, Dad . . .!"

"I've got my method of cooking them, and that's what people like."

"Yes, but—"

"No buts," said Lenny. "When you're a bit older, we'll move you on to the burgers."

"I dink murgh smwr blarr grreff riff frawy!" said Edith, reappearing.

"Pardon?" said Lenny.

"Pardon?" said Benny.

"Sorry, my mouth was full," she said, wiping her face with one of **Lenny's Burgers** serviettes (available also at the side of the van). "I said, I think you should let him do that right away. These hot dogs are fantastic!"

And with that, she was gone, running as fast as she could – which wasn't very fast, it was more like a very stiff sped-up walk – towards the football ground. Benny looked up at his dad hopefully.

"Hmm," said Lenny. "Well, OK. Maybe next game."

Benny's eyes widened. "Do you promise?"

"Yes, Benny. I promise. And a promise is a promise!"

"Thanks, Dad!" said Benny, grinning from ear to ear.

"I SAID, BURGER, PLEASE, MATE! HELLO?"

CHAPTER 3

Benny, since he was a very small boy, had always wanted to be a chef. But he didn't come from a background that made him feel as though he could ever actually end up as one. When he saw chefs on TV or online – even the ones who spoke with accents that made them sound like the men asking loudly for burgers at the van – they all seemed like people who lived in really big houses with incredibly sleek kitchens. And they all had loads of shiny saucepans and blenders and ladles and spatulas and knives and every possible ingredient you could ever want, to cook anything, waiting for them in their cupboards.

Benny's kitchen at home was different. It was small, very small – more of a corridor off the living room than a separate room. It had an electric cooker and a little fridge. They had three saucepans that had once been silver but were now mainly brown, and two non-stick frying pans, both of which now had many bits of food stuck to them. As for ingredients, it was all Benny could do to get his dad to buy salt. And when his father did do that, it was always a big sack of salt that could be used for gritting the road, not one of the many exciting varieties of chef's salt – sea or chilli or something called kosher – that Benny sometimes saw on Juliana Skeffington's show.

Juliana Skeffington was his hero. She had a TV show, but Benny had loved the way she cooked from well before that had happened, from when she had

just been one of the millions of people online filming themselves cooking and sharing their recipes. He loved her because even though she was famous now – and like all the other famous chefs had a big, amazing kitchen – when she'd started she had been in a tiny space a bit like his own, using pans that looked worn and tired, also like his own. Plus, she had a very nice face and friendly smile, and she had a catchphrase, which he really liked. She would look into the camera whenever she finished a new dish and tasted it – she often closed her eyes in pleasure for a moment and then opened them again – and say: "And remember – cooking isn't just about food: it's about love." Benny knew it was kind of corny, but he still really liked it when she said it anyway.

He had watched Juliana cook all sorts of dishes from nearly every part of the world: beef bourguignon, chicken tikka masala, paella, spaghetti carbonara, spring rolls, jerk lamb, falafel, Brazilian fish stew, ramen, gazpacho, ratatouille, kebabs and many others. Benny knew he'd never be able to reproduce these amazing recipes in his own tiny ingredient-starved kitchen, but he loved watching her make the food anyway. He would always make sure – via his dad's social media account – to like her videos, and, in the comments, to say nice things about everything she cooked.

Benny's dad would watch him watching the videos and smile. Despite being an actual cook, Lenny was not interested in cooking. Even though cooking did run in the family. Lenny's father-in law, Benny's grandad on his mum's side, Kenny, had also

been a cook.[6] Kenny had run a restaurant, a long time ago. Well, a restaurant is probably pushing it: it was a café, called **Kenny's**.[7] But **Kenny's**, by all accounts, was a great café. It was known as what is called a greasy spoon, which doesn't mean its spoons were greasy[8] but that it specialised in foods like full English breakfasts and sausage sandwiches and, indeed, burgers. It had been very popular, and when the time came for Kenny to retire, Lenny, along with Benny's mum, Rose – thank heaven she hadn't been named Penny – took over running it. Sadly, not long after that, right after Benny was born, Rose died in a car accident. Lenny tried to keep the café going, partly in memory of his wife, but he became depressed, lost most of his joy in cooking, and eventually **Kenny's** was sold – for a lot less than it was worth – to a much bigger business.

6 Benny came from a long line of people called names like Kenny, Lenny and other Bennies, who he may or may not have been named after.
7 Lenny shared with Kenny a laziness as regards spending a long time thinking about anything, like names of food outlets.
8 Although some places that are known as greasy spoons do have greasy spoons, so don't use this book as a restaurant guide.

These days, Lenny was less depressed, but the sadness sometimes threatened to overwhelm him. Nor had he wanted to run a café any more. But greasy-spoon cooking was all he knew how to do, so he ran a burger van. Hence **Lenny's Burgers**.

As a tribute to the memory of Benny's grandad, a memento always sat on a shelf in the van, the one next to where the food prices – Hot Dog £4.99, Burger £5.99 – were written up on a blackboard. It was a book. It was a hardback and had probably once been a sketchbook, but Kenny had used it to write down his recipes. **Kenny's** hadn't served that many different dishes, but Kenny had added little drawings and details about the recipes, along with quite a few dishes that he perhaps had hoped to make one day but never got round to. Which meant that inside there were more than enough pages to justify the title written on the front in careful handwriting: Kenny's Cookbook.

Sometimes, when getting into the van, Lenny would open Kenny's book and think about the cook he could have been. Every time he opened it, looking at the handwriting and the pictures – starting to fade now – there was a moment that was almost magical. But then, always, he would realise the time, that the Bracket Wood fans would soon be clamouring for burgers and hot dogs, and shut it again.

CHAPTER 4

"A Big Bonkers, please!"

"OK. You want to make that a Bonkers Banquet?"

"Er, what do I get for that?"

"A Bonkers Beverage . . ."

"Sorry?"

"A drink."

"Oh."

"And a Bonkers Bowl."

"Sorry. What's that?"

"Either a salad or some beans."

"Bonkers Beans?"

"No, we don't call them that."

Jasper blinked. "Seems like you've missed a trick there . . ."

"What?" said the **Bonkers Burgers!** woman behind the counter. Her name, according to the badge on her red uniform, which was decorated all over with BBs, and exclamation marks – **BB! BB! BB!** – was Margot. She wore a hat with a red visor. This also had the **BB!** logo on it: the face of a small smiling bear (the **Bonkers Burgers!** bear, who was called Bonkers) plus the **BB!** slogan, which was "WHEN YOU'RE BONKERS FOR A BURGER, IT HAS TO BE . . . A BONKERS BURGER!" That (being bonkers, crazy, wacky, silly or kooky) was the brand of **Bonkers Burgers!** – a fast-food chain that had actually trademarked its name to include an exclamation mark. It was also where Jasper – a good friend of Benny's – was presently ordering.

Margot didn't look bonkers, crazy, wacky, silly or kooky. She looked tired and bored. She glanced at the queue behind Jasper, which, this lunchtime, was very long.

"Well . . ." said Jasper, adjusting his glasses, as he liked to do when explaining something because he thought it made him look clever, "surely if everything else that begins with a B on your menu is preceded by the word bonkers, then beans should be as well, no? Hmm?"

Margot stared at him blankly. "Do you want the Bonkers Banquet or not?"

Jasper stopped adjusting his glasses. "I think . . . no."

"Right," said Margot, turning round. "Big Bonkers!" she shouted.

"Bonkers Big!" the cooking staff behind her shouted back.

"Why do you think they say that?" said Benny, as Jasper stepped back to join him and their other friend Mina, who was waiting a bit behind him in the queue.

"What?" said Jasper.

"Big Bonkers . . . Bonkers Big!"

"It's a catchphrase. They say it whenever anyone orders a Big Bonkers," Jasper explained to Benny.

"Yes, but why?" said Mina. "It doesn't mean anything . . ."

"Bonkers Big!" came the shout again from the

cooking staff as another one was ordered.

"That's all part of the bonkerness of **Bonkers Burgers!**" said Jasper, who was a big fan of **Bonkers Burgers!** and didn't like to question any element of it – even though he had just questioned why the beans weren't called Bonkers Beans. But that was only because, secretly, he felt he could work at **Bonkers Burgers!** to help make it even more bonkers.

"Seventy-three!" said Margot.

"That's me!" said Jasper, beaming, and went over to the till.

"Have a Bonkers Day . . ." said Margot, handing over his Big Bonkers. Everyone at **Bonkers Burgers!** said that when they handed over the food. They were meant to say it in a very upbeat way. Which was not how Margot said it.

"Are you not having anything?" said Mina to Benny.

"No," said Benny. He lowered his voice to a

whisper: "Don't tell Jasper, but I don't really like Bonkers burgers."

"I think he might have worked it out," Mina whispered back. "What with you never having one."

Benny smiled. "I've brought a sandwich that I made at home, following a Juliana Skeffington recipe."

"Oh," said Mina. "Let me guess . . . Parma ham with Gruyère? Roast chicken with homemade chilli mayo? Crawfish salad with lemon?"

"Well done!" said Benny. "Those are indeed all real Skeffington sarnies. But no – we don't have any of those ingredients at home. So when I say a Juliana Skeffington recipe, what I mean is . . ." He took a foil packet out of his bag and waved it in front of her. "Cheddar and onion, but kind of made how I think she would make it."

"With love?" said Mina, smiling.

"Exactly," said Benny.

"Yes?" asked Margot blankly. Mina and Benny had now reached the front of the queue.

"A No-Beef Bonkers, please," said Mina.

"Don't do those any more," said Margot.

"Pardon?"

"Don't do 'em. Discontinued. Last week."

"Oh," said Mina, disappointed. "Why?"

"Dunno," she said. "Ask Bodley Bonkers."

"Who?"

"Bodley Bonkers!" said Jasper, holding his open carton and staring at his Big Bonkers. "He's the CEO of **Bonkers Burgers!**"

"CEO?" said Benny.

Jasper frowned, but still didn't look up from his burger. "Complete . . . Exact . . . Owner," he said. "I think. He started all this from a small burger place himself. He was the chef, you know."

"Have you got anything else that's vegan?" asked Mina.

Margot pointed up at the very brightly lit menu above them. "We've got what's up there."

Mina and Benny looked up. On the menu were some very large photos of burgers, including the Big Bonkers, the Double Big Bonkers, the Brilliant Bonkers (a Big Bonkers with Bacon), the Really Brilliant Bonkers (a Big Bonkers with bacon and cheese), and the You're Bonkers Mad You Are Bonkers (a double Big Bonkers with bacon and cheese).

Mina – who had very sharp eyesight and read very quickly – said immediately, "They aren't vegan, though. Or vegetarian?"

Margot frowned. "There's the Chick-O-Bonkers."

"That's made with chicken, isn't it?"

Margot looked at her blankly. "Yes?"

Mina sighed. "I'll have a Berry Bonkers Beverage, please."

Margot nodded and punched something into the

till. She glanced over at Benny. "You?"

"Nothing, thank you," he said.

"Have a Bonkers Day," she said flatly.

CHAPTER 5

"I just don't get it," said Jasper, holding up his Big Bonkers, out of which he'd already taken a large bite. "These are just so great. Why do we even come here if you don't like them?"

"Because you like them, Jasper," said Benny.

"And because I like the No-Beef Bonkers," said Mina. "Well, I liked them. When they had them." She took a disconsolate[9] sip of her Berry Bonkers Beverage, which was in a cup that was

9 Sad. But with an element of annoyance too.

bigger than their heads.

"Never had one of them," said Jasper, taking another bite of his burger. "Which is something. I've tried every single Bonkers burger. But not that one."

"Because . . .?" said Mina.

"No beef. Says so on the tin."

"They don't come in tins," said Benny, who was finishing his cheese-and-onion sandwich, which he'd cut beautifully into quarters. "They come in Styrofoam cartons."

"It's something my dad says. It means: it is what it says it is. And a no-beef burger has no beef in it. And –" he opened his mouth for another big bite – "I like beef."

"You know it's not beef, right?" said Mina. "Beef is just a word we use so that we don't think of what we're eating as what it is." She pointed at the half-eaten patty between the sesame bread roll of his Bonkers burger. "A cow."

Jasper frowned, as if what Mina was saying had genuinely never occurred to him.

"A cow, by the way," she went on, "that will have had a horrible life before it was horribly—"

"OK, OK," said Jasper, holding up his hand. "I know what you're trying to do. But it won't work. You can't put me off my Bonkers burger. Not possible."

"To be honest," said Benny, "I'm not entirely sure that Bonkers burgers are made from cows."

They both looked at him.

"Pardon?" said Mina.

"Well . . ." he said, also pointing to Jasper's half-eaten burger, "proper beef should be marbled with fat. It should be, when cooked, a lovely deep-brown colour. And a burger should be a thick slab, not a thin round brick."

"Bricks aren't round," said Jasper.

"I didn't know what else to compare it to," said Benny, continuing to point at the patty. "It should be cooked medium rare. Not burned to a crisp."

"It's not crispy."

"Yes, I know. That's also wrong. It should be. Crispy on the outside and juicy on the inside. The sauce . . ."

"Oh, we're also throwing shade on my sauce now?"

"The sauce should be a mix of tomato ketchup, mayonnaise, mustard and lemon juice . . . hand mixed and spread evenly over the meat, not –" his finger moved closer to Jasper's burger, to where a pink glob of **Bonkers Burgers!** sauce was looking almost lonely next to a limp bit of lettuce – "processed out of a big vat and splodged on. And let's not even get started on the –" he raised his fingers, making speech marks in the air – "salad."

Jasper shook his head, but then he smiled. "Both of you are not, however hard you try, going to put me off my Bonkers burger!" He opened his mouth wide, deliberately baring his teeth.

Suddenly Benny reached out and grabbed the burger out of Jasper's hand.

"Hey!" said Jasper.

Mina laughed. Benny stood up. He stood up, in fact, on his chair.

"Ladies and gentlemen!" shouted Benny, holding up the burger. "Let me explain something to you!" The other diners in the restaurant turned to him. "What is this?"

There were murmurs and:

"Eh?"

"Who is that?"

"Shut up!"

"What?"

"OK . . ." Benny continued. "Yes! It looks like a burger. It smells . . . kind of . . . like a burger. And there're lots of photos around this place of similar burger-like objects. I can see on the menu they are all called burgers." He held up the Big Bonkers, or what was left of it, even higher. "BUT THIS," he said, "IS NOT A BURGER."

Jasper rolled his eyes. Mina smiled. She knew that Benny was a bit like this – a bit likely to do and say the first thing that came into his head, when he felt inspired to do so. It felt sometimes sort of dangerous, but at the same time exciting.

"Thank you for your attention! Enjoy your non-burgers!" Benny cried.

He jumped down and

handed the Big Bonkers back to Jasper, who was shaking his head slowly. Mina did a small clap, to which Benny bowed.

And then, to his surprise, he heard more people clapping. He looked around. All the staff who worked at **Bonkers Burgers!** had come out from behind the counter and were applauding. They were standing in front of the tills in their red BBs! uniforms and actually clapping. Some of them were even cheering.

Benny was surprised. He had only been doing the speech to show off to Mina, who he secretly really liked (like, really liked). But if the staff at **Bonkers Burgers!** liked what he was saying this much, he thought, maybe things in here . . . maybe they could start to change – and the cooking could become different, more infused, like Juliana Skeffington always said with love and—

"Wow!" said Margot. "I can't believe it."

"Thank—" Benny began to say, but he never got

to "you". Because someone else – who he hadn't seen come in while he was making his speech – interrupted.

"That's OK, Margot," said a calm American voice.

Benny looked round. Standing at the door of **Bonkers Burgers!** was a short man, dressed in a very smart suit and tie. He was also wearing a **Bonkers Burgers!** hat – the same kind with the visor and slogan as all the staff. Which made him look weird. And he was grinning. Really grinning.

Behind him were two very large, very frightening-looking people – one man, one woman – in slightly less smart suits and dark glasses. They were not wearing hats.

"That's OK, all of you," continued the man. "I'm just dropping in, as I like to do so from time to time – visiting random stores to see just how bonkers things are at a particular branch of **Bonkers Burgers!** I am – as we say at Bonkers HQ – bonkers like that! But don't you worry. I —" and here he drew himself up to his full (not very high) height — "Bodley Bonkers —" he paused, then nodded, as if taking in that everyone was very impressed with him being Bodley Bonkers — "can see that everything is completely bonkers here!"

CHAPTER 6

"Particularly," Bodley Bonkers continued, still grinning and turning towards the table at which Benny and his friends were sitting, "over this way!"

"Oh my days!" said Jasper. He got up and ran towards Bodley. Immediately, the two very large people stepped forward, forming a shield in front of the **Bonkers Burgers!** CEO. They each held out a single hand, palm up.

"Steady," said the man.

"Steady," said the woman.

"That's OK, Michael, Michaela. Don't worry," said Bodley, pushing through them, with some difficulty.

"Yes!" said Jasper. "Don't worry, big bodyguards! I just want to tell Bodley how much I love **Bonkers Burgers!** And how much I'd like to work here one day!"

Bodley beamed at him. "That's nice, little boy. I'm sure that could happen. Margot!"

"Yes, sir?" said Margot, running forward and seeming to curtsy as she did so.

"Get the little boy a hat! Pronto!"

Margot frowned. She looked around helplessly, as if wanting to say, *Um, but we don't have a large stock of spare hats* . . . Then her face relaxed and, reaching up, she took off her hat and handed it to Jasper.

"Thank you!" he said. He turned back to Bodley. "I was thinking more . . . you know . . . design . . . brand management . . . big ideas . . . but . . ." He put the hat on his head. "This is great!"

"Mm-hm," said Bodley. "But it wasn't actually you, my friend, that my eye – and ear – was taken by."

"Oh," said Jasper.

"No," said Bodley, brushing past him, followed by Michael and Michaela, which meant that Jasper was very brushed aside. "It was more . . ." And now he was standing by Benny; he was, in fact, pointing down at Benny's head. "THIS GUY!"

"Oh," said Jasper again.

"Really?" said Benny nervously.

"YES!" said Bodley. "I mean, what a hilarious funny speech that was! Ha ha ha ha ha ha ha!" he said. He did actually say "ha ha ha". It sounded much more like he was saying something than . . . laughing. "About our burgers not being burgers. Oh my," he went on, wiping his eyes, although there

didn't seem to be any tears there. "You know what
that is? BONKERS. It's the most bonkers thing I've
ever heard!"

"Oh," said Benny. "Right. It wasn't really meant to
be a joke, though."

"HA HA HA HA HA!" said Bodley, now sounding like he was shouting the "ha"s, but still not sounding like he was laughing. "Even funnier!"

"Er . . . Mr . . . Bonkers?" This was Mina speaking.

"Yes, little girl?"

"Well, I'm eleven, so . . . Is your surname actually Bonkers?"

"Never mind that," said Bodley, and he stopped grinning for the first time since he'd arrived.

"OK . . ." said Mina, looking a bit worried. "What I really wanted to say was . . . Why have you stopped doing the No-Beef Burger?"

"Aha! I'll tell you why, little eleven-year-old. Not bonkers enough!"

"Pardon?"

"No beef. Not bonkers!"

"Right," said Mina. "What does that even mean?"

"HA HA HA HA HA HA!" said Bodley. "Also, they didn't sell as well as the others. Anyway, look – the point is, well done for your joke . . . What's your name, boy?"

"Benny. Benny Burns."

"Kenny Burns? Not the Kenny Burns who we forced to . . . No, of course you can't be."

Benny frowned. "No, not Kenny. Benny. Kenny was my grandad's name."

"Of course it was! How BONKERS of me! You're eleven. I mean, Kenny – he'd have to be . . ."

"He's dead."

"Right. HA HA . . ." Bodley began, and then stopped, realising that ha-ha-ing might not be appropriate here. "ANYWAY . . ." he said loudly, with a sense of moving on. "Brilliant."

"What, my grandad being—"

"NO! The joke. About the Bonkers burger not being real," said Bodley.

"Well, as I say, it wasn't—"

"I mean, they are unreal. In a way. Yeah? They're

so good they're unreal. AREN'T THEY?" Bodley said, looking around.

The staff who had been standing watching Bodley's conversation with the children – although some of them seem to have drifted off – snapped back to attention and applauded.

"YEAH!" said Bodley, punching the air. He put his arm round Benny. "You know what I'm saying!"

"Not re—"

"Have a Bonkers Day!" said Bodley, and with a nod to Michael and Michaela, who flanked him immediately, out he went through the automatic doors of **Bonkers Burgers!**

CHAPTER 7

"OK," said Lenny. "Big moment. Big Saturday. Big match day. But most importantly, Small Fry – the big day we move you up to burgers!"

Benny nodded excitedly. He already had his whites on. You couldn't see how white they were, because it was dark in the burger van with the shutter down. But it was nearly noon, and that was when Lenny was going to unlock the shutter and the customers would start flocking to **Lenny's Burgers**.

"I hope you're up for it," continued Lenny. "You've been out at your friends' houses all week, so I do hope you're not too tired! Anyway, *how do we cook the burgers?* you may well ask."

"Well . . ." said Benny.

"What you do, son, is you take the patties out of the freezer, you press 'em on the grill, cook 'em till they're nearly black on one side, then the other, then—"

"Dad."

"What?"

"I'm not taking the patties out of the freezer."

"You're not? Where are you going to get them from? The cat's bottom?"

This – the cat's bottom – was somewhere Lenny often referred to when he was being, as he was now, sarcastic. It annoyed Benny – not so much because it was a bit gross, but because they didn't even have a cat.

"No." He opened the fridge, which stood beside the freezer, where normally they only kept milk – although why they kept milk no one knew, as no customer had ever, in the history of **Lenny's Burgers**, asked for a cup of tea or coffee. He bent down and took out a tray. On it were ten well-rounded pink circles. He showed the tray to his dad.

"What are these?" asked Lenny.

"Beef patties," said Benny.

"Eh? But we've got loads of burger patties!" said Lenny, opening the freezer. And indeed they had: there seemed to be hundreds of them in there, piled up on top of each other, wrapped not very tidily in cling film. "I buy them in bulk on the first of the month, without failure, from that freezer shop. You know, the one named after the cold country. What's it called again?"

"I know. But . . . I've been making my own. To a different recipe."

Lenny frowned. "Recipe? Making your own burgers? I've never bothered with that."

"Well . . . yes, Dad. I know." He nodded at the tray. "But these are different. I've added stuff. Herbs. Spices. And I don't put them in the freezer; it dries them out. And—"

"Hold on, hold on, hold on," said Lenny. "I said we'll move you up to burgers. I didn't say anything about making them differently!"

"I know, Dad. But I . . . I want to make them differently."

Lenny took a deep breath. "Are you saying . . . my burgers taste like—"

"No . . ." said Benny before his dad could go any further.

"Hundreds of Bracket Wood fans eat them every Saturday!" said Lenny, looking – and sounding – pained. "So far, no complaints!"

"Well . . ." said Benny.

"All right, not no complaints."

"I think at the last count it was seven."

"OK. But only one of them actually ended up in hospital!"

"I'm not saying my burgers will be better. But I did use . . . Well, I did base them on –" he glanced over at the shelf a little nervously – "Grandpa Kenny's recipe . . ."

Lenny looked round. On the shelf was sitting, as ever, Kenny's Cookbook.

"Really . . .?" said Lenny.

"Yes," said Benny.

Lenny frowned. "I don't remember giving you permission to take the cookbook down from the shelf." He went over to it and carefully picked it up. "It's old now and we need to be careful with it," he said quietly.

"I was," said Benny. It was true. He had been allowed to see it before, of course, but only with his dad turning the pages. This time, though, while his dad had been out buying frozen patties in bulk, Benny had stayed in the van and, daringly, taken it down and looked at the recipes and drawings by himself.

To get it down from the shelf, he had stood on the same box he used to cook on the grill. Then he had sat cross-legged on the floor, just about able to make out the pencilled scrawls on the pages in the low light of the van. It had been exciting, partly because he knew he was being a bit naughty, but also because he had felt like some kind of archaeologist hero, unearthing an ancient manuscript covered in strange hieroglyphics[10].

"Really, Dad, I took a lot of care."

Lenny looked back at him. He shrugged, indicating that if the book hadn't been damaged, he wasn't that worried about it. He put it back on the shelf. "OK, Small Fry."

10 Mysterious writing, like the ancient Egyptians used on the walls of the pyramids.

"Dad?" said Benny, after a pause.

"Yes?"

"I used the secret ingredient," said Benny. "The one on the first page."

Lenny looked at him and smiled.

"Ah," said Lenny. "I see. The secret ingredient. Well, in that case, I assume these patties are going to be amazing!" He looked down at the tray. "But where did you even make them?"

"At Jasper's house."

"Oh, right. Our kitchen not good enough, I suppose?"

"Well . . . no."

"You're supposed to deny that!"

"Sorry."

Lenny looked again at the tray. "Well. We can. If you must. Serve them. I mean, no point in wasting food. But –" he let out a laugh – "I don't think – how many is it, ten? – they're going to last a whole afternoon. So . . ." he said, turning back to the freezer, "whatevs. We'll soon be going back to the regular ones."

There was a knock on the side of the van.

"Who is this now?" said Lenny. He went to the side door and opened it. Standing there, holding two trays of patties each, were Mina and Jasper.

"Hello, Mr Burns!" said Mina.

"Eh?" said Lenny, as they stepped in. "When have you been making all these?"

"All week," said Benny. "That's what I've been doing at my friends' houses!"

"We always have a lot of mince in our kitchen . . ." said Jasper.

CHAPTER 8

It took a little while, but it happened.

Eventually, after Benny's friends had invaded his van, Lenny gave in and let Benny mastermind the burgers. Every time someone in the queue shouted out "Burger!" he nodded to his son, who took a patty off the tray and put it on the grill. He also did something that had never happened in **Lenny's Burgers** before, which is when a cheeseburger had been ordered, just before the burger had finished cooking, Benny would glance at Jasper, who was nearby holding a plate of sliced cheese, and he'd peel off a square of mild Cheddar and lay it carefully on the hot patty. When, and only when, the cheese had melted perfectly, he would flip open the roll, toasting next to it, and slide the burger inside.

Meanwhile, at the sauce table, there was something else. Mina was standing by, with a red squeezy bottle. This contained a burger sauce that Benny had also made during the week, with – as he had explained in his little speech at **Bonkers Burgers!** – mayonnaise, tomato ketchup and lemon juice. To each Bracket Wood FC fan who appeared with a burger, she would offer a splodge of sauce. Most said yes. She also offered something else that had never, up to this point, been part of the **Lenny's Burgers** brand, which was a bit of lettuce, a slice of tomato and, expertly cut into small circles by Benny, a few pickled cucumbers. Most said yes to these as well.

At first, apart from these apparently small changes in the burger-making process, everything was normal in and around the burger van. Fans queued up. They shouted for their food. Someone asked for chips, which someone always did, even though **Lenny's Burgers** had never done chips. It was business as usual.

Then Edith, who had turned up early, to make sure that she avoided the rush of the previous Saturday – and who, to prove to Lenny that she could overcome her superstitions, today had ordered a burger instead of a hot dog – suddenly came back to the van.

"Lenny! Lenny!" she was shouting.

"What, Edith?" said Lenny, irritated and certain that she had returned to complain.

"The burger! The burger!"

Lenny looked to his son, who was taking a short break from cooking, holding a fizzy drink. "If she hated it, Small Fry, it's all over. I'm afraid . . ." he whispered.

Benny gulped the drink down, concerned.

"I'm sorry, Edith," said Lenny. "Whatever your issue is . . . the thing is – call me a softie, a silly dad – but I decided today to let Benny cook the burgers. Sorry – you can have your money ba—"

"Yes! I know! And . . ." She held up in her hand a tiny bit of food. Benny could just make out that it was the last bite of one of his cheeseburgers. "It's brilliant. It's amazing. It's the best burger I've ever tasted!"

"Oh!" said Lenny.

"Oh!" said Benny. "Thank you!"

"Although, to be honest," said Edith, "I wouldn't know. Until today, I've only ever had hot dogs."

"Oh," said Lenny.

"Oh," said Benny.

And that might have been that – and dismissed by

all as Edith being a little bit bonkers burgers herself – were it not for what happened next. Which was a man in a Bracket Wood FC vintage[11] top coming out of nowhere and saying, "Yes! Me too! Mine was delicious!"

And then a woman in a tracksuit, who had just started eating a burger, saying, "Oh Lord, I've never eaten one as good as this!"

And then a couple, who had split their burger in half, saying together, "We love this!"

And then, most amazingly, a man who wasn't even a Bracket Wood fan – he was wearing red and green, the colours of Bracket Wood's great rivals, Oakcroft Athletic, who they were playing that day – came over and said, quietly: "I don't like to say this about one of the enemy's burger vans, but my personal rivalry as a fan has simply been overridden by the taste of that meaty delight. Well done to you, and please don't tell any Oakcroft fan that I've said

11 From 1971, the year they had made it to the fourth round of the Southern and District Local Semi-Pro Cup competition. This was Bracket Wood FC's record footballing achievement.

this." And with that, he left.

Lenny looked at Benny and said, "Blimey. I think you may be on to something!"

Benny smiled, but not for long. Because in front him all he heard was:

"Burger, please!"

"Burger!"

"Burger for me too!"

PART TWO

CHAPTER 9

"OK!" said Bodley Bonkers. "I call to order this meeting of what I like to call the **Bonkers Burgers!** Top Brass . . ."

A blonde woman, sitting at the table in front of him, blew a long note on a toy trumpet.

"Yes, thanks, Milly!"

She continued to blow it.

"Very good, Milly!"

She took a breath.

"Yes, I wonder if the next item on the agenda might be to cancel that particular bonkers idea . . ." said Bodley.

PAAAAAAAAAAA!

"Stop! Just stop!"

Milly took the trumpet out of her mouth.

"Sorry, Mr B, I couldn't hear what you were saying because—"

"You were playing the toy trumpet, I know."

"Such a bonkers idea of yours. To play that every time you say the words Top Brass," she said. "Just one of your many brilliantly bonkers ones!"

"HA HA, yes," said Bodley. He looked round the table – a long, polished wooden one in the centre of the meeting room on the top floor – the fortieth – of Bonkers & Co. Inc. LLP Ltd[12]. Floor-to-ceiling windows along two sides of the room showed a view of the skyline. At the table sat:

Milly Mackay, his Head of Planning,

---

12 I don't know what all these combinations of letters mean either.

Shazad Smith, his Head of Development,

Nick Norbert, his Head of Food and Drink,

and

Sarah Sherbet, his Head of PR.

All these words – planning, development, PR, even food and drink – aren't important. Milly, Shazad, Nick and Sarah's seats at the **Bonkers Burgers!** Top Brass table were only, in truth, about one thing: saying yes to Bodley Bonkers. OK, two things. Saying yes to Bodley Bonkers and laughing at his jokes.

"Anyway," Bodley continued. "I call this meeting of the Top—"

PAAAAA!

"SHUT UP!"

Milly put the trumpet down.

"The people at the top of the company," said Bodley carefully, "because I want to know how we are doing. I expect the usual report of . . ." He paused and looked to his Top Brass.

As one voice, they said: "BONKERS BRILLIANT!"

"Yes, I expect we will be doing . . ." He paused again.

"BONKERS BRILLIANT!"

". . . across all sectors, in every single branch, as ever, but I guess there's no harm in going over the figures. Milly?"

"OK, thank you, sir."

"Just Bodley. No sirs or madams in this room."

"OK, thank you, Bodley."

Milly got up and went over to a laptop. "Can you shut the blinds, please, Nick?"

"Um . . ." said Nick, who wore glasses and had a very pointy nose, "think that's not really my job."

"Well, it's no one's job," said Shazad. "We don't have an official blind-shutter!"

"HA HA HA HA HA HA!" said Bodley. Then to Sarah: "That was a joke, right?"

"Come on, Nick – don't be a pill," said Milly.

"Oh right," said Nick, getting up, with a sour face. "It's always me who shuts the blinds. It's never Sarah. Or Shazad. Or you, Milly!"

"Actually," said Sarah, "I did it in the last meeting."

"Oh," said Nick. "OK." He shut the blinds. The room got darker.

"Right," said Milly. She tapped a key on the laptop. On a big screen at the far end of the room, some graphs appeared. They were normal-looking graphs, although in the corner of the screen there was a little animated figure of Bonkers (the **Bonkers Burgers!** bear), which smiled and clapped every time a new graph showed up.

"Well," said Bodley. "I can see all the lines going up, up and up. Which is . . ." He paused, frowning. "I said, which is . . ."

"Oh, do we still do it even in the dark?" whispered Shazad.

"I guess so," whispered back Sarah.

"I SAID WHICH IS . . ."

"BONKERS BRILLIANT!" said the Top Brass.

"So," said Milly, "that's the end of the presentation, I guess—"

"Hold on," said Bodley. "Wait one moment."

He got up and walked over to the screen, squinting against the light. Being a small man, he had to crane his neck to look up at it.

"What's going on with this graph?" he said.

Milly looked over. "Oh, the Bracket Wood branch?"

"Yes, the Bracket Wood branch. Why is it not going up? In fact, it seems on a regular basis to be –" he squinted harder – "going down."

Milly looked at the graph. "Oh, yes. That's odd.

Once a week, it seems. On Saturdays. There's a drop-off. Why would that be?"

Bodley turned to her. "I'd say that's your job to know."

"Is it?" said Milly. "I'm Head of Planning."

"Yes!" said Bodley. "And it's not in the plan of **Bonkers Burgers!** to have a drop-off at any branch ever!"

There was a silence, except for the animated face of the Bonkers Bear on the screen, smiling and clapping.

"I think," said Nick, opening the blinds, "I might know what it is . . ."

"OK," said Bodley.

"So . . ." said Nick, "in Bracket Wood, next to the football ground, on Saturdays, there's this burger van . . ."

"It's a thing in this country, Bodley," said Sarah, leaning over to him. "Burger vans. Outside football grounds. On Saturdays."

"I know that, Sarah. I live here," said Bodley. He turned to Nick. "There have always been burger vans outside that football ground. What's changed?"

"I'm not sure. Maybe the cook in a particular van. This one."

Nick held up his phone. On it was a photo of a burger van. Written on its side was **Lenny's Burgers.**

"That?" said Bodley. "That's our competitor? How do you know?"

Nick adjusted the picture, zooming out, and held up his phone again. This time the photo showed not just the van but the queue for the van: a long, long queue. It seemed to go on for miles.

"Wow . . ." said Sarah.

"Wow . . ." said Milly.

"Wow . . ." said Shazad.

"Yes, enough with the wows, already," said Bodley. "Why is the queue so long?"

"Because the burgers are really good," said Nick.

Bodley stared at him. "Oh. They are, are they?"

"Um. . . yes . . ."

"And how would you know that?"

"I . . . um . . . well, firstly, I'm a big Bracket Wood FC fan."

"You are?' said Bodley. "You've never mentioned it before."

"Oh, yes. Come on the . . ." Nick seemed to be looking around for help. There was quite a long pause.

"Brackets," he said eventually.

"Right. And the burgers?"

"Well, obviously I'm not going all the way there just for the burgers. I mean, that would be silly."

"Yes," said Bodley. "It would be especially silly, given that there is a **Bonkers Burgers!** outlet – the Bracket Wood branch that we're discussing, in fact – just at the end of your road, isn't there?"

"Ha ha, yes!" said Nick, and, suddenly spying what he hoped was an opening, continued: "I'm not that bonkers!"

"Mmm," said Bodley, not laughing. "I see. Did you queue up? For the burger?"

"Yes. I'd heard they were very good, you see."

"Had you."

"Yes."

"And . . .?"

"And what?"

Bodley sighed. "Was the burger you bought as good as you'd heard?"

"Yes. Um. It was delicious."

Bodley nodded. Nick had gone a bit white, although his pointy noise had gone red, at the point. Bodley approached him.

Everyone in the room sensed what might be coming next. Which was:

"More delicious, Nick, would you say –" Bodley

stepped very close to him, peering up at his pointy nose but clearly trying his best to look his Head of Food and Drink in the eye – "than, perhaps, a Big Bonkers?"

"Um . . ." said Nick.

"Um," said Bodley, turning away. "I'll take that as a yes, then."

"No!" said Nick.

"No? No, it wasn't as nice as a Big Bonkers?"

"No, of course not."

Bodley nodded. He didn't take his eyes off Nick. "In what way?"

"In every way," said Nick quickly.

Bodley raised an eyebrow. "Well. I see. For someone who is my Head of Food and Drink to be a little . . . vague . . . I would have thought you, Nick Norbert, would be much, much more able to elucidate—"

"Eluci-what now?"

"To describe exactly the many, many ways in which the taste of a Big Bonkers is superior to a greasy, grotty, grubby, stale suspect-meat sandwich from a football burger van. Perhaps you could do that . . . right now."

Bodley stepped back and folded his arms.

Nick's face went even whiter. But he took a deep breath, and said, "I can. I can do that. Yes. So . . . a Big Bonkers is much nicer than that burger I got from that van because . . . because . . . because . . . ooooooohhh my!" And Nick collapsed in a heap on the floor.

Sarah Sherbet, Milly Mackay and Shazad Smith ran over. Bodley just watched as they knelt, saying, "Nick! Are you OK?" and "Do you need some water?" and "Call a doctor!"

"He hasn't really fainted, has he?" said Bodley.

"I have!" said Nick from within the huddle of his fellow Top Brass. He did at least sound faint. "That was a real faint! I didn't just pretend to faint because I couldn't answer the question! What kind of person would that make me? Oh, I feel faint again."

"OK," said Bodley. "I think I need to go and see what's going on at this burger van."

CHAPTER 10

"A Benny burger, please!"

"Yes, and for me!"

"We'll have four, thanks very much!"

Business at **Lenny's Burgers** was booming. It was booming, as you may have guessed, because of the burgers cooked not by Lenny but by Benny. So much so that the said burgers were now being asked for by name: not "A burger cooked not by Lenny but by Benny please" but – as you've just heard – "A

Benny burger, please!" His burgers had, in the space of a few weeks, become what people call a thing. Fans of Bracket Wood FC would turn up, sometimes a couple of hours early, looking forward not just to the game – and with it some singing and shouting – but also a Benny burger. It had become part of the experience.

The running of the van had undergone some changes. Lenny, now that he was making good money from his son's talent, had changed his tune about who was the better cook in the family, which meant that Benny no longer had to make the patties secretly at Jasper's house. Lenny bought all the ingredients Benny needed, and Benny made them at home. Jasper and Mina still came to the van on Saturdays to help though, because there were so many customers.

It was mainly regular customers, but every Saturday the number of regulars grew, as people far and wide started to hear about this legendary burger they had to try. Today, there were more than ever, and they all wanted a Benny burger. Lenny, in fact, now spent most of his time working for Benny, rather than the other way round – handing him trays of patties, taking orders, sorting change and just generally giving his son the time and space to cook.

As Lenny took yet another order, a new customer who very much didn't look like a regular suddenly appeared. He was barging through the queue, with the help of a rather large man and woman, who were shoving the other customers out of the way.

"Oy!"

"What you doing?"

"Look out!"

Those and more shouts came from the queuing customers, but to no avail. The newcomer kept on ploughing through till he reached the burger van.

He was dressed like a football fan, but one who'd

been told how to dress like a football fan and then got everything wrong. For a start, he was not wearing the right colours. Indeed, he was not wearing any specific colour. On his head was something red: a fluffy red top hat. On his torso was something yellow, which was also the wrong colour and wasn't a football shirt: it was a puffa jacket. Underneath that was something green, which sadly was still not a football top, but may have been a rugby shirt. On his legs he had something orange: these were shorts, which is kind of a football thing but not normally worn by fans. They were very long though, and may just have been trousers that were a bit too short. Which was odd because the customer himself was quite short.

He also had a moustache, which was very clearly a false one, and a pair of glasses that were pink and looked like they had no lenses in them. The large man and woman he was with, however, were wearing black suits. Although they had adorned them with scarves, neither were for Bracket Wood FC but for Oakcroft Athletic.

"Bricket Forest, Bricket Forest, Bricket Forest!" chanted the man. "Come on, everyone!" he said,

turning to the queue, who were frowning at him and looking confused. "What's the matter with you?" He grabbed the large woman's Oakcroft Athletic scarf, held it above his head, then sang: "And it's Super Bricket Forest! Super Bricket Forest FC! We are the most bestest football team the world has ever had."

He stopped singing and looked back at the queue. "Still no one joining in?" He shook his head. "I guess I'm just too much of a superfan for some people."

His voice was odd. It sounded like someone trying to sound like a bus driver. To be more specific: it sounded like an American trying to sound like a British bus driver. Which meant he was mangling the words in all sorts of ways.

"Anyway!" he continued in the same strange voice. "I hear that if you're a real fan of Bricket Forest FC, this is the place you gotta come for your pre-match burger. Would that be correct?"

Lenny stared at him. "Um . . . well, it's one of the places," he said.

The man frowned. He looked at the large man in the suit.

"I thought you said this was definitely the place?"

"It is the place. I think he's just being humble," replied the suited man.

"Being what?"

"It's the place," the suited man said again.

"OK!" said the man wearing all the wrong colours. Then he turned to Lenny. "Give me one of your special amazing burgers!"

Lenny squinted at him. "Do you mean . . . a Benny burger?"

"Is that what they're called? Yeah, I suppose so."

"Yes, but you need to get in the queue, mate. You can't push in like this."

This seemed to totally confuse the man, who looked round as if the very idea of a queue had never been explained to him before.

At which point, a voice said, "Hold on, aren't you Bodley Bonkers?"

CHAPTER 11

The man turned round. Standing next to him was Edith, wearing, obviously, all the correct scarves.

"Who?" said Lenny.

"Bodley Bonkers!" repeated Edith. "The bloke who runs **Bonkers Burgers!** I saw a photo of him in the paper once."

"I really hope you aren't him. I am not at all keen on him. Or his company," said Lenny darkly.

"No, I am definitely not him," said the man, now seeming a little worried. "Not at all."

"Oh, that's good," said Edith. "I didn't like the look of him in any way. He had a very annoying face. Really quite difficult to look at."

"Right," said the man. "Well, there we are . . ."

"It made me feel ill."

"Did it?"

"Yes. Also very annoying, I'd add, were some of the things he was saying in the paper. About how wacky and zany everything is at **Bonkers Burgers!** That was all very silly. And also annoying."

"YES, YOU SAID THAT!" the man replied quite loudly. "NO NEED TO SAY IT AGAIN!"

"All right," said Edith. "Keep your hair on. Although . . ." she said, stepping back and looking suspiciously at his hair as if it might be a wig, "I'm not sure that's all that easy for you."

"Here you are, sir!" said Benny.

The man turned to the burger van, his face red and angry. Benny was standing on his box, holding out a burger. But not just any burger. It looked almost like the Platonic ideal of a burger[13]. The sesame-seed bun seemed to be cradling its contents within a soft embrace. The edges of the patty had been seared to a golden brown, and, lapping over the corners (from a Cheddar square placed on the patty while grilling) were perfect

melted triangles of cheese. The accompanying fillings – a crisp tear of lettuce, a slice of plump tomato, a sprinkling of pickles, plus an attractively pink dollop of sauce – looked fresh and delicious.

And the smell: smoky and savoury and deeply hunger-inducing. The man went quiet. His anger vanished. He stared at it.

13 This is a very complicated concept and frankly I don't know why I've put it in a children's book. But basically it means that if in your mind you have an ideal image of a burger, one that perfectly suits what you think a burger *should* look like, this was it.

"Is that a Benny burger?" he said huskily.

"That's what people round here are calling it!" said Lenny proudly, putting an arm around his son. "Cooked by my Small Fry here!"

"Yes, sir," said Benny, handing it over. "Do eat it while it's hot."

"Right," said the man. He took the burger. He bit into it.

For a moment, nothing happened. And then he could feel himself falling. Not actually falling physically, but falling inside, down, deep down, to a place where the man – who, as you have perhaps guessed, was indeed Bodley Bonkers – had not been for a long time. A place where he felt warm and safe and sleepy and happy. A place he could only be brought to by taste. A taste as luscious and juicy and tangy and complex – the burger was somehow sweet and salty and spicy and smooth and creamy and crunchy and everything in between – as this.

Bodley Bonkers stayed there, rooted to the spot, in front of **Lenny's Burgers**, holding the burger. He stayed there, his eyes shut behind the lensless glasses, for a long time – long after he had swallowed that first mouthful. Finally, he opened them. He saw all the other burgers, cooking away on the grill in front of Benny. Then he noticed, behind the young boy, up on a shelf, a book – and handwritten on its spine were the words **Kenny's Cookbook**. He peered at it. And he peered some more. It seemed to offer him something – a secret – a key to what might be the taste that had just transformed him into a pillar of bliss; a way of how to get there himself, rather than coming here, pretending to be something he wasn't.

He wanted that book. And when Bodley Bonkers wanted something, he usually got it. He even reached out a hand towards it, into the van.

But then Lenny said:

"Would you mind moving away now, sir . . .? We've got a lot of other customers . . ."

CHAPTER 12

Later that same day, after the match had ended, fans were drifting away from The Bracket. Most of them were looking a bit depressed, because, as usual, Bracket Wood FC had lost. Benny and Jasper and Mina and Lenny, however, were not depressed. It had been another good day's business. They had washed up the grill, sorted out the inside of the van and put boxes of cooking equipment into Lenny's car. Lenny drove away, waving happily. The children began walking home, which they liked to do after a hard day's cooking.

"It's going so well!" said Jasper.

"Yes. Although that guy – the one in the pink glasses and all the wrong colour scarves – was a bit weird . . ." said Benny.

"He liked the burger though," offered Jasper.

"He didn't say that."

"Yeah, but I could tell."

"OK."

Benny looked over to Mina, who wasn't saying anything. She seemed to be deep in thought.

"All OK with you, Mina?"

"I was wondering . . ." She turned to him. "I like helping out in the van, Benny. I really do. And it's very nice of you to put me on sauce and salad duty, so I don't have to handle any meat . . ."

"Well, it's really nice of you to help at all."

"But I was wondering . . . I know this might be

difficult – and I know your dad would have to pay to get the new patties – but what if we could offer a plant-based alternative?"

"A what-the-what now?" said Jasper.

"You know what I mean," said Mina, sighing. "A plant burger. A vegan burger."

"Um . . ." said Benny.

"You can get really good ones now," said Mina. "Ones that you can't even tell the difference . . . from a—"

"A real burger?" said Jasper a bit sneerily, a bit like "this is clearly impossible".

"Well, yes. Although the dictionary definition of burger is – I checked this out on my mum's computer – 'a flat round cake of a savoury ingredient'. And a vegan patty is definitely savoury. So there's nothing to say that the meat burger is the real burger, any more than the vegan one."

Jasper snorted. "Yeah. Like anyone thinks that."

"Thinks what?" said Mina.

"That a burger is a cake. I mean, where's the icing?"

"All right, Jasper," said Benny, laughing. "I think maybe step away from this argument. I'll try and speak to my dad about it, Mina. I mean, he's only just accepted the idea of me cooking the burgers. I don't know how he'd feel about introducing a vegan one . . . I'm not sure he'll think it's really the sort of thing the average Bracket Wood FC fan fancies for a pre-match snack."

Mina smiled in spite of Benny's words. "Well, if anyone could cook a vegan burger to change their minds about that, it's you."

But Benny looked doubtful. He wasn't convinced that she was right. He didn't say this out loud, because he didn't want to upset his friend, but in his heart he didn't believe that, even with his cooking skills, he could make a vegan burger taste as good as a beef burger. Although he had a lot of sympathy with Mina and what she believed about animals and not eating meat, another part of him just really wanted to carry on proving that he could cook the best burgers in Bracket Wood.

"OK, I'll definitely think about it," he said,

while silently he couldn't help wondering, Why change a winning formula?

CHAPTER 13

A few days later, Benny and Jasper were leaving their school, Bracket Wood Primary. At the same moment, a group of seven adults were walking down the road towards them.

"Isn't that—" said Jasper, but before he could finish the question, Bodley Bonkers, who was at the front of the group, said, "Hi! How you doing?"

"Me?" asked Jasper.

"No, the other guy."

"Me?" repeated Jasper.

"That's just you again. Stop speaking. No, I want to have a chat with –" and here he came over and put his arm round Benny – "this guy! The Burger Boy of Bracket Wood!"

As he said this, the other grown-ups – which included the man and woman in black suits, who were looking extremely suspicious – all nodded their heads. Some of them said "Yes!" and "Way to go" and "Hoo-hoo!"

"Hello," said Benny. "It's . . . um . . . good to see you again."

"Yes!" said Bodley. "Because we met last week, didn't we? At the local branch of **Bonkers Burgers!** AND NOWHERE ELSE . . ."

"Right. Although we did have a customer at the van on Saturday who looked very like—"

"AS I SAY, NOWHERE ELSE." Bodley coughed. "No. I've just heard about your burgers, young sir. In fact, I've heard good things. Very good things."

"Well, thank you," Benny said politely, taking Bodley's arm off his shoulder. "Anyway, I really must be—" As he tried to move away, he was stopped by the two bodies of the very large man and woman, who stood in front of him.

"Keep an eye, Michael," said the woman.

"Got him, Michaela," said the man.

"Hello," said a younger man from the group. "My name is Nick Norbert. I am Head of Food and Drink at **Bonkers Burgers!**"

"Wow!" said Jasper. "Can I have a selfie with you?"

"Really? Well, I suppose so . . ."

"NO, NORBERT!" said Bodley.

"No, no, of course not. Anyway, Benny – you are Benny Burns, correct?"

"Yes," replied Benny.

"I have been authorised by Bonkers and Co. Inc. LLP Ltd . . ."

"What do all those letters mean?" asked Benny.

"Well, they mean . . ." Nick turned to the group. There was a lot of shrugging. Nick shook his head and continued: "A lot of important stuff. Anyway, the point is: we at the company are prepared to offer you a sum of money in return for your recipes, specifically for those relating to the ingredients, creation and/or presentation of your, um, burgers."

"Pardon?"

Bodley moved forward. He smiled. His teeth were very white. "We'll pay you, Benny, a very generous amount of cash, in return for your burger recipe."

"Whoa!" said Jasper. "How cool is that? Think about it! Everyone will get to try your burgers!"

Benny frowned. He didn't know what to say to this. His instinct was just to tell them: "Thank you very much, but no thanks." But then another voice appeared.

"Sorry, what are we all talking about?"

Benny looked round. It was his dad, Lenny, come to meet him from school.

CHAPTER 14

"Hello there," said Bodley. "And who would you be?"

"I'm Lenny Burns. Benny's dad."

"Aha! The actual owner, I believe, of **Lenny's Burgers**!"

"Yes."

"And I imagine that you, sir, would be interested in a little cash injection to your business . . ."

"Well . . ." said Lenny, looking a bit uncomfortably at Benny. "Maybe . . ."

Sarah Sherbet leaned forward, holding a file. She took a piece of paper out of it. "We've drawn up a tiny contract. We were going to offer it to Benny to sign, but obviously you would be better, as his parent and legal guardian."

She handed it over. Lenny glanced down at it, then he looked up.

"A thousand pounds . . ." he said.

"Yes!" said Bodley. "Imagine what you could do with that!"

"Dad . . ." said Benny.

Now Milly Mackay stepped in. "We would require that you hand over any recipe books you may possess."

"Oh," said Lenny. "Right."

"But what a result!" said Bodley, beaming. "A thousand pounds for a handwritten cookbook that's just sitting on the shelf of your van!"

"Sorry," said Benny. "How do you know about that?"

Bodley's smile disappeared.

"HA HA HA HA HA HA!" he said.

"Pardon?" said Benny.

"Don't know why I laughed," replied Bodley. "Anyway, we really must be getting on. So . . . Shazad?"

Shazad Smith took a step forward, and held out a pen and cheque.[14]

"As you can see, sir," he said to Lenny, "here is the thousand pounds. I've already had it made it out in your name."

"Right," said Lenny. "This is all a bit quick."

"Yes, Dad," said Benny. "Can we go home and talk about it, maybe?"

"Oh, no, no, no, no, no!" said Bodley. "This is a once-only offer. We don't have time for long negotiations . . ."

"Can I still keep making my burgers in the van afterwards?" said Benny, starting to sound a little desperate.

14 You don't see these much any more. They are bits of paper with promises on them to pay people money. They were all the rage in the twentieth century.

"Oh, that's all covered in the small print," said Nick Norbert.

"Yes, it's very small," said Lenny, bringing the contract up to his face and squinting.

"Yes, you don't have to worry about it," said Bodley airily. "It's just blah, blah, blah. The sort of thing that you have to have in all contracts!"

Benny tugged at his dad's jacket. "I'm really not sure about this, Dad."

"You might not be sure, Small Fry," said Bodley, coming closer, "but I think—"

"Sorry," said Lenny. "How do you know his nickname?"

Bodley looked at him blankly. "Er . . . I just guessed." There was an awkward pause. "Anyway, um, Benny . . . You don't really understand what a thousand pounds can do for your family. Do you?"

Benny stared at Bodley. He shook his head sadly. He looked a bit like he was going to cry.

"The pen again, please, Shazad," said Bodley.

Bodley's Head of Development proffered the pen – which had a picture down the middle of it – to Lenny.

Lenny took it. The pen's nib hovered above the contract. Then he frowned.

"Sorry is that . . . a bear? On the pen?" said Lenny, peering at it.

"Yes," said Shazad. "It's Bonkers! Our mascot! We have him on all our merchandise!"

"He's so great!" said Milly.

"Such a sweetie!" said Nick.

"I love his little face!" said Sarah.

"Yes, yes, he's super great," said Bodley. "Can we get on?"

"Bonkers?" said Lenny. "Are you from **Bonkers Burgers!**?"

The men and women looked at each other.

"Well, yes," said Bodley. "Didn't we make that clear?"

Lenny clicked the nib back into the pen. "No. I just thought you were . . . some businessmen. And women."

"Well, we are," said Milly Mackay. "But from **Bonkers Burgers!**"

"Yes," said Lenny through gritted teeth. "And ten years ago you basically forced me out of business!"

Sarah looked confused. "When?"

"When you made me sell you **Kenny's**! Benny's grandad's caff!"

Bodley Bonkers frowned – and smiled at the same time. "I don't think so, Mr Burns. As far as I remember, **Kenny's** . . . wasn't quite working out for you, so we helped you out by buying the building off you. And in its place we set up a new **Bonkers Burgers!**"

"You didn't help me out!" said Lenny, going quite red. "You paid me next to nothing for it, and your lawyers forced through the sale!"

"Excuse me," said Nick. "I think we may have to sue you for saying that—"

"Do!" said Lenny. He threw the pen to the ground. It broke in two, leaving a rather sad image of Bonkers' face, looking up without the top half of his furry head, which was about a metre away. "I'll see you in court!"

With that, he yanked Benny away. Jasper, who as we know was a big fan of **Bonkers Burgers!**, shrugged apologetically, but followed.

Bodley, in front of his entourage, watched them go.

"I think, ladies and gentlemen," he said loudly, so that Benny and Lenny and Jasper could hear, "this means war."

CHAPTER 15

Despite this foreboding announcement, for the next few days nothing happened. There was no sign of Bodley marshalling troops to attack the van, or bombs being dropped on it from **Bonkers Burgers!**-branded planes flying high above, or Benny being kidnapped from school by men in masks and forced to work in the **Bonkers Burgers!** kitchens.

Maybe, Benny thought, *Bodley's forgotten about it.*

Which meant he had time to visit Dottie. Mina

had been talking to him about Dottie for a while – about how nice she was, and how much she thought Benny would like her – and so, while things were a bit quieter around the van, he'd said, "Yes, OK – I'd be happy to meet her."

And there was no doubt that Dottie was a lovely cow. This may sound odd – but just because an animal is not a dog or a cat or a rabbit, or any other animal that everyone thinks makes a cute pet, doesn't mean they can't have personalities. Before this, Benny had never really thought about what a cow might be like to get to know, but Mina had clearly been right: Dottie was lovely.

The two of them were standing, on a Saturday morning, in a field at Bracket Wood City Farm. The city farm didn't have many animals. It had four sheep, three pigs, two llamas, and a cow: Dottie. Dottie was a very placid cow, and so Benny and Mina were allowed to stand in the field with her.

She rumbled over to them slowly and looked up at Benny with her big . . . well, cow eyes.

"Is it OK . . . to stroke her head?" he said to Baku, a woman who worked there and who had taken them out to the field to meet Dottie.

"Yes," Baku said, laughing, and she did so herself. Dottie seemed to purr under Baku's hand. OK, she didn't purr – cows can't do that – but she looked very contented, and said "moo" very quietly.

"Mooo . . ." said Mina.

"Are you talking to her?" said Benny, laughing.

"Kind of."

"Moo," said Dottie.

"Oh, she's answered back!" said Benny.

"Yes. I think she understands."

"Understands what?"

Mina blushed a little. "That I'm her friend who's come to see her."

"Mina comes here all the time!" said Baku. "The

animals love her, especially Dottie. OK, I have to go and check on stuff in the office – we have some money worries, boringly, which we need to sort out – but I'll leave you two with her. Enjoy." With that, she headed out of the field.

Mina put her hand on Dottie's head. Benny put his hand on it too. Her head felt warm and slightly furry. She licked her lips.

"She's really nice," he said.

"Yes," said Mina. "She's kind of a rescue cow."

"Hmm . . . I haven't heard of that. I've heard of a rescue cat or dog but . . ."

"Yes, well, those are the animals that people think of as needing rescuing. But Dottie was a dairy cow, which meant that when she had babies . . . calves . . . they were taken away from her, and then she was used to produce milk for humans."

Benny tried to think about this. He found it difficult.

"And then she was going to be killed, for meat," continued Mina. "But this farm managed to rescue her from that. Which is why she's here."

"Right . . ."

Dottie gazed at him again. Benny couldn't tell if there was any meaning to her look. But, even so, he could only see friendliness in her eyes.

"And . . ." said Mina, "I think that when you actually meet cows – or pigs or sheep – and you spend a bit of time with them, you start to realise that they're . . . well, they're basically just people in a different form . . . They're the same as us; they just can't speak, at least not our words . . . Then it feels really weird that we kill them and eat them."

Benny looked at Mina. She wasn't hectoring him. She wasn't making a big speech designed to make him feel bad. She was just saying what she thought.

He could feel something shifting in him. Her words were making him think harder about . . . everything. Well, not everything. What Mina was saying, and what Dottie's eyes were making him feel, it was all making him think harder about—

"The van!"

Benny looked up. It was Jasper, running to them across the field.

"What?" Benny called out.

"Come back! To the van! Now!"

CHAPTER 16

When the three of them arrived back at the van, Benny noticed straight away that something was wrong.

"Dad . . ." he said. "It's an hour until match time. Where's the queue?"

"I don't know!" said Lenny, looking out at fans passing by on their way into The Bracket. "I don't know what's going on?"

"OK, OK," said Benny. "Well . . . maybe it'll get

better soon. Let's just wait."

But twenty minutes later – with Mina and Jasper standing by with their trays and sauces and salad – there had been exactly zero customers. Even Edith hadn't come for her hot dogs. Benny thought he had seen her running quickly past the van into the stadium, as if not wanting to be seen by him and his dad, but he wasn't certain.

"This isn't right," said Lenny.

"No," said Benny.

"Benny," said Mina. "Does Bracket Wood FC have a mascot?"

Benny frowned. "I'm not sure . . ."

"They used to have Brackets," said Lenny.

"Brackets?" said Benny.

"Yes. It was a character that looked like a pair of brackets."

There was a pause.

"What was that costume like?" said Jasper.

"It was basically a man holding two toy bows out by his sides. One each side of him."

Jasper seemed confused. "Bows?"

"As in 'and arrow'."

Another pause.

"How did that work?" asked Benny.

Lenny shook his head. "It didn't really. Anyway, I haven't seen him around for a long time."

"OK," said Mina. "Then who's that?"

She pointed into the distance, towards the other end of the street. They all craned their necks to look. Where there appeared to be a bear. Handing out leaflets.

CHAPTER 17

"Really?" Benny heard a man say. "Free?"

"Yes. Absolutely free!" said the bear, and handed the man a leaflet. The man scurried off, licking his lips.

The bear itself was, in fact, one of three bears – though there was no sign of anyone playing Goldilocks – handing out leaflets around the area of Lenny's burger van. Benny noticed that each bear – and by bears, it should be clear, we are talking not about carnivoran mammals of the family Ursidae[15]

---

15 This is what it says on the internet that bears are. Obviously I didn't just know this.

but people dressed in cartoon bear costumes – had been positioned to form a triangle, a kind of net, in which the burger van was caught.

Benny approached one of them. "Can I have one of those leaflets please . . .?" he said, and the bear handed one over.

Benny looked down at it. It was a **Bonkers Burgers!** leaflet. It said:

On the leaflet, there were various pictures of burgers and bears and cartoon people laughing. Benny noticed the asterisks, after "SATURDAY" and "HERE". He checked the bottom of the page, where, much like the contract offered to his dad, there was some small print.

*Only available between the hours of 1 p.m. and 6 p.m., and no other time.

By "here", we mean the Bracket Wood branch and nowhere else in the **Bonkers Burgers! universe.

Benny took the leaflet back to the van. They all read it. They had a lot of time to do so, as no one was ordering any burgers.

"Hmm," said Lenny. "Well, I don't think this is a coincidence."

"Neither do I," said Benny.

"Neither do I," said Jasper. "Because I don't know what 'coincidence' means."

"It means something that's happened by chance,"

said Lenny. "Which, as I say, this isn't. **Bonkers Burgers!** have put this offer on deliberately, on match days, in this area only, to try and drive us out of business! Just like they did to **Kenny's**!"

"That's awful," said Jasper. "Meanwhile, can I see that leaflet again . . .?"

Benny handed it to him. Jasper didn't look at it, but instead said, "Actually, I've just remembered . . . My mum wanted me to get home early today to . . ."

"To . . .?" said Benny, as Jasper was already stepping away.

"To . . . have tea!"

"Right," said Benny. "Do you think you'll manage it though, after you've eaten your free Big Bonkers?"

But Jasper was gone, running in the direction, indeed, of **Bonkers Burgers!**

"What shall we do?" said Mina.

"I don't know," said Lenny. "We can't afford to give away burgers."

Benny could see his dad's shoulders sagging in sadness, and he said quickly, "There must be something we can do. After all, we know much more about the people who support Bracket Wood FC than **Bonkers Burgers!** There must be something about that knowledge that we can use!"

"What though?" said Lenny. "And, even if we did, how would we scupper what **Bonkers Burgers!** are doing?"

"Excuse me," said a voice. They turned round. It was a bear. Well, it was a man in a bear suit, presently holding a bear's head. It was, in fact, Nick Norbert, Head of Food and Drink at Bonkers & Co. Inc. LLP Ltd, in a bear suit, holding a bear's head.

"Yes?" said Lenny.

"Could I, um . . ." Nick said in a whisper, looking round furtively, as if he might be spotted, "have a Benny burger?"

CHAPTER 18

"HA HA HA HA HA HA!" said Bodley Bonkers, sounding, perhaps for the first time, as if he was genuinely laughing. "I didn't expect them to give up this easily! But of course they have! No one takes on **Bonkers Burgers!**"

"Ha ha, yes!" said Nick Norbert, doing his best to laugh like Bodley and not really succeeding. They were back on the fortieth floor of Bonkers & Co. Inc. LLP Ltd. Nick was showing another slide on the screen. The blinds had been shut. By him. "So, just to go over what happened, I went to the burger van – not to get any of their food, of course – why would I want to do that? Don't be silly – who even made that suggestion? So I went to apply a bit of pressure at a time when I knew they would be under the cosh."

"Good work," said Bodley.

"And Benny Burns – clearly realising that fighting us was a waste of time – said that he would give me the recipe for the sauce. Not for the whole burger yet, but I'm sure that's on the way . . ."

"I'm sure it is!" said Bodley.

Nick clicked on to another slide. It showed a burger split in half. On top of the patty sat the sauce, which was . . . slightly strange-looking. " As you see," said Nick, "from the sample we've already made up, it's a very red sauce. In fact, it's red and white. He said it's very important that we don't mix

138

the ingredients too much. He said to make sure that the sauce is on the patty in blocks of red with streaks of white in it . . ."

"Easy!" said Bodley. "Our state-of-the-art kitchen technology can create that – no problem!"

"And to celebrate this," Nick continued, "we're going to package our free Big Bonkers in cartons in the same colours. Red and white stripes!"

"That's a great idea!" said Shazad Smith. They all agreed it was.

"Whose idea was that?" said Sarah Sherbet.

"It was Benn— mine!" said Nick Norbert.

"Bennmine's?" said Milly Mackay.

"Sorry, no I was just coughing. Before I said the word 'mine'."

"That's an odd cough," said Milly.

"Yes. Benn! There – I've done it again." Nick paused. "But the idea was definitely mine!"

"Right, well," said Bodley Bonkers. "That's enough

meeting chat. This is a company that does; not a company that talks!"

"Is that a new slogan?" asked Shazad.

"No, I just said it. But the point is: let's get on to it. Let's make those burgers and those cartons and put them out there for next Saturday! And that, I think, will be the end of our battle with –" Bodley's mouth curved into a delighted sneer – "Benny's burgers!"

CHAPTER 19

"BOOOOO! BOOOO!"

"Help! Help! What's happening?"

"BOOO!"

"I want to run away!"

"You can't! The doors are locked!"

"BOOOO! **BONKERS BURGERS!** BOOO!"

Things hadn't turned out quite as planned. The person saying "Help! Help! What's happening?" was Nick Norbert, once again dressed in a bear costume, and once again holding his bear head. Only this time he was cowering inside the Bracket Wood branch of **Bonkers Burgers!** along with Milly Mackay and Shazad Smith, also in bear costumes and holding bear heads. They all looked terrified.

"It's best that they stay locked!" continued Margot, the server, who was at the doors looking out at the crowd massed behind them.

"But why are they so cross?" said Milly.

"BOOO!"

The boos were accompanied by the sound of Styrofoam cartons being thrown at the doors and windows of **Bonkers Burgers!** Notably, the new Styrofoam cartons that had been coloured in red and white stripes.

"I did say this," shouted Margot over the boos,

"when we got the instructions from head office for this new burger promotion. In these colours . . ."

"Say what?" said Nick Norbert.

"I said that these are the colours of . . ."

"**We hate Oakcroft and we hate Oakcroft! We hate Oakcroft and we hate Oakcroft! We hate Oakcroft and we hate Oakcroft! We are the Oakcroft haters!**"

". . . Oakcroft FC," continued Margot, quietly, as the chant stopped for a second. "Who are Bracket Wood's main rivals . . . who they are playing today?"

Milly Mackay and Shazad Smith looked over at Nick Norbert.

"Oh," he said. "I didn't know that."

The crowd, eventually, began to move away. The bear-costumed leafleteers watched them go. Many of them seemed to be heading in the direction of **Lenny's Burgers**. Where there was already a large queue forming.

"I think, Nick Norbert," said Milly Mackay, "that you've been played. By an eleven-year-old boy."

CHAPTER 20

For a while everything went back to normal. Business at **Lenny's Burgers** was good again. Demand for Benny burgers was again creating long queues before Bracket Wood games. Then suddenly, one day, the queue was gone again.

Benny looked out from the van, trying to see if there were people in bear costumes handing out leaflets as before, but there was no sign of anything like that.

In fact, there was no sign of anything – except supporters milling about, all avoiding the van.

Suddenly Benny saw Edith scuttling by. She seemed to be holding something in each of her hands, which meant that she was scuttling without moving her arms much, which looked quite strange. It also meant that she wasn't scuttling that fast, so Benny was able to nip out of the door of the van and catch up with her easily.

"Hey, Small Fry," said Edith, still scuttling, and still holding her arms down.

"Hello, Edith," said Benny. "You not getting a burger or any dogs today?"

"No. Nothing. Absolutely nothing today, thank you."

"Are you sure? I could do you a double Benny burger? As one of my favourite customers, I'll do it for the same price as a single . . ."

"Look, Benny!" she said. "I don't know how to

make this clear to you. Today, I just don't want –" to emphasise her point, she raised one of her hands to point a finger at Benny's face – "a hot—" She stopped speaking. Because she wasn't pointing a finger. She was pointing a sausage. From one of the hot dogs she was holding.

Uselessly, as it really wasn't helping to emphasise the point any further, she raised her other hand. In which there was also a roll, which held a sausage.

"—dog," she said.

"OK, Edith," said Benny. "What's going on?"

Four minutes later, Benny was back at the van. There had still been no customers.

"What's going on?" said Mina.

"Edith bought her hot dogs from one of the other vans."

"Why? She always comes here!"

"Dad. Can I borrow your phone for a minute?"

Lenny frowned, but said, "Sure," and handed it over.

Benny tapped it a few times, then – with a grim face – said, "She told me it was because . . . Yes. Look at this."

He turned the phone to face them. On a very well-watched social media platform was a short reel. It showed a man – a man who they knew well, for it was Nick Norbert, head of Food and Drink at Bonkers & Co. Inc. LLP Ltd – on the toilet. He didn't look very happy. He looked very white and very sweaty. As he faced the camera, his voice was hushed.

"Hello."

"You don't need to say hello . . ." whispered a voice from behind the camera. It sounded very like Shazad Smith's.

"Oh. Sorry."

"Don't say sorry."

"Sorry. Um. Anyway." Nick adopted a dramatic

voice. "This is a warning. A warning to anyone who might be thinking about buying a burger or a hot dog or any food at all from a van called **Lenny's Burgers** . . . that stands outside . . . Bracket Wood FC . . . and . . ." He gasped and frowned, squeezing his face up. "Oh dear. Hold on." The film seemed to cut and jump. Then it was back again.

Nick stared at the camera. "Yes, what was I saying . . ."

"**Lenny's Burgers** . . ." hissed the camera voice. "God."

"Yes. **Lenny's Burgers**. I bought a burger there, and yes, it looked nice – oh, yes – and it tasted nice, so very nice . . ."

"OK, don't overdo it," said the voice.

"Um. Right. Yes, anyway. I ate it. And to cut a long – very long – story short, I've been sitting here on the toilet ever since. So . . ." Nick's face started to contort. "Urrgh . . . Don't eat there! Don't buy anything there! Don't . . . aaargh! END UP LIKE ME!"

He was waving his hands at the camera as he said this. Then the screen went black.

"Hmm . . ." said Lenny. "Not very Christmassy." (This was something Benny's dad said about anything he didn't like, whatever time of year).

"No."

"But how come Edith saw it?" said Mina. "How many people follow his account?"

Benny glanced down. "Not that many. But —" he held up the phone again, pointing to a specific name underneath Nick Norbert's account — "it's been promoted by the **Bonkers Burgers!** account! Which has ten million followers."

"Which means it's been viewed . . ." said Jasper, looking at the screen, "seventy-eight million times."

"Oh," said Benny.

"Oh," said Lenny.

"Oh," said Mina. "But hold on a minute . . ." She

peered at the phone, with her very sharp, very fast-reading eyes. She pointed a finger at a corner of the screen. "What's that?"

CHAPTER 21

"Hello," said Benny Burns. "I'm Benny Burns. I'm only eleven, but every Saturday I cook burgers and hot dogs at this van, **Lenny's Burgers**, which is owned by my dad. Last week, a man called Nick Norbert – who works for **Bonkers Burgers!** – posted a video of himself on the toilet." He started laughing. "Sorry."

"Benny!" said Mina.

"Sorry, I can't say 'on the toilet' without laughing."

"OK . . ." said Mina, scribbling something down on a piece of paper. "Try saying this instead."

She handed it over. And then called out, "Take two!"

She was holding up Lenny's phone, using it as a camera, while Benny was standing in front of the van. He repeated what he'd just said, but this time, when he got to the toilet bit, he said instead: ". . . Nick Norbert – who works for **Bonkers Burgers!** – posted a video claiming that he had got food poisoning from one of our burgers. But one of my friends, Mina . . ."

Mina turned the phone round. She waved into camera and said "Hi there!" before turning it back to Benny.

"She noticed something about his video . . ."

"Next to Nick Norbert," Benny's voice continued – only now they were back inside the van, watching the video they had made, and the screen now showed a frozen image of Nick Norbert on the toilet, "if you look closely . . ."

The camera zoomed in on the image. A little red circle – Mina's handiwork again (she was good with technology) – formed just to the side of Nick Norbert's feet and crumpled trouser legs. On the floor next to him was a medical carton, which said on the packet: LAXOFORM. And underneath that: MAXIMUM STRENGTH.

"Well, you can see that he's taken some pills, which –" and here you could hear that Benny was suppressing another laugh – "have made him poo a lot. This seems a strange thing to do if you've eaten something that's already making you –"

yet another suppressed laugh –" poo a lot."

The video then switched back to Benny outside the van. "Anyway. I'm just an eleven-year-old kid who loves cooking and helping his dad and his business . . ."

Lenny shuffled into shot. He didn't seem to know what to do, so he just stood there and did a thumbs up.

"We just about survive selling burgers in a van every Saturday," Benny went on. "We check our meat very thoroughly, and I'm pretty sure our burgers won't poison you, so don't believe the rumours you might hear – and . . ." Lenny passed him a paper plate, on which there was a Benny burger. Benny held it up. "Come and get one of these! Next time you're in Bracket Wood! And, um, thank you."

They stopped the video.

"OK," said Lenny. "I'll post it. And then we just have to wait and see if it has any effect."

*

Some time later, they checked to see how many times their video – entitled "Benny Burns Reacts to **Bonkers Burgers!** Takedown of **Lenny's Burgers!**" – had been watched.

"Um . . ." said Mina. "Five times."

"Right," said Lenny. "Sorry. I don't have many followers."

"How many do you actually have?" said Jasper.

"Five."

"Right. So I guess they've all watched it. At least."

"Yes," said Lenny.

No one said anything for a moment. Then Lenny sighed.

"Look, everyone," he said. "I think you all did really well with this. And it makes the point brilliantly. And we should be allowed to fight back against **Bonkers Burgers!** if they're spreading lies about us. But we just don't have the reach that they've got. So maybe we've just got to admit that we've lost . . ."

156

No one said anything again. Benny made a face, a face that might have been an attempt to stop himself not laughing this time but crying. Lenny got up to shut the van's shutters. Inside everything went dark.

"Oh!" said Mina, who was the only one still looking at Lenny's phone, the light from which was shining up on her face.

"What?" said Benny.

"We just got another view . . . and another. Oh! It's going up really fast!"

"What's happening?" said Jasper. "How?"

Mina peered at the screen. "It's been liked. And reposted on her feed! And she's got even more followers than **Bonkers Burgers!**"

Benny stared at her. "Who? Who are you talking about?"

Mina smiled and turned the phone to show him. "Juliana Skeffington!"

CHAPTER 22

A few days later, **Bonkers Burgers!** made a public statement. They posted it on their social media account, the same one that had been sharing Nick Norbert's toilet video – which had now been taken down.

APOLOGY

The management and staff at **Bonkers Burgers!**, and everyone at Bonkers & Co. Inc. LLP Ltd, would like to apologise, very deeply, for a video that was recently shared by our account, implying that the burgers cooked by Benjamin Burns at the **Lenny's Burgers** van in Bracket Wood are dangerous to eat. It was posted by an employee, who has since been sacked. The employee in question was acting completely on his own behalf and had not, definitely not, been instructed to create such a video by senior management. In particular, he had not been told, as some rumours have suggested, that he had to post this video – which, much to everyone at Bonkers & Co.'s disgust, showed him on the toilet – in order to resolve a problem that he himself had created via a promotion of delicious Big Bonkers burgers packaged in red and white colours, which, on a previous occasion, caused some resentment towards our company among fans of Bracket Wood FC. That is not true and we will take legal action against anyone who continues to perpetuate such rumours. However, meanwhile, we at **Bonkers Burgers!** are only too pleased that young chefs like Benjamin Burns are keen to try their hand at cooking burgers and wish him every success.

"We should frame that!" said Lenny, looking at the same announcement in the local paper, after a very, very good day's business for **Lenny's Burgers**.

Following the reposting of Benny's video on @ JulianaLovesFood, the whole episode had blown up on social media, with lots of people posting messages in support of Benny. There was even, briefly, a hashtag: #IStandWithBennyBurns – and then #ILoveBennysBurgers – which trended across the internet. This meant that when Lenny and Benny opened up the van on the following Saturday, they got customers not just from among the usual Bracket Wood supporters but from far and wide. People who clearly had never heard of Bracket Wood FC, or perhaps even the Southern and District Local Semi-Pro League at all, were queuing for a Benny burger. This was obvious because they weren't wearing Bracket Wood colours, but also because they were saying things like "I stand with Benny Burns" as they handed over their £4.99.

"Yes," said Benny, although he thought to himself

that he would rather frame the words of support that Juliana had sent him in a private message to his dad's account. She'd written:

Hi Benny. You might not realise it but I check my accounts regularly, and I know that you've been a wonderful fan of my work for some time, and so when I saw that you'd started cooking and you needed a bit of help, I thought I should repay the favour. Much love Jx

At that moment, Benny was staring at that message again and was lost in wonder, thinking he could read it and read it again and again, forever.

CHAPTER 23

Bracket Wood City Farm was normally a peaceful place to be. But today there was unease in the air. The pigs were snorting in a strange anxious way. The sheep were running around as if being chased by an imaginary sheep dog. The llamas were shedding their wool. Even Dottie, who was usually serenity personified[16], was blinking a lot and mooing in a way that didn't sound happy at all.

"What's going on?" said Benny.

16 A posh way of saying "very calm indeed".

Mina shrugged.

"I think they've picked up on the fact that I'm worried about something," said Baku.

"What is it?" said Mina.

Baku shook her head. "It's just a money thing. We rely heavily on donations here. But times are tough now for lots of people, so we haven't been getting many donations recently. The bills are piling up." She looked down. "I try not to get too uptight about it, because the animals . . . they're so . . . they can feel what I'm feeling. I don't know how they do it. But they always seem to know when I'm worried."

Her phone went, and she frowned. "OK, sorry, I have to take this," she said, and went away.

Mina looked to Benny. "I don't know what we can do about that . . ."

"Neither do I," said Benny. "But she's right, isn't she? It's like the animals know."

Mina looked out at the field. She nodded. "Yes,

I think so. My mum says there's a word for that: empathy."

"What does that mean?"

"It's a bit like sympathy, but deeper, I think. It means that you can imagine what someone else is thinking and feeling. People believe that only humans can do that. But that's not true."

Benny nodded. His face hardened a little. He turned to her and said, "You're right, Mina. Everything you've always said about eating animals. It's weird. It's weird that we just think that's OK. That's it." He drew himself up to his full height, and announced, as if telling the very creatures most concerned: "I'm going to cook non-meat burgers from now on."

Mina looked shocked. "Well . . ." she said. "Hold on a minute. I don't want to make things difficult for you. Or your dad."

Benny smiled at her. "We can do it. What you said to Jasper was right. You can get plant burgers now that are so good people won't even be able to tell the difference."

"Yes, but . . . I just thought maybe you could offer them as an alternative. You don't have to stop cooking meat ones completely."

Benny looked at Dottie. "But as long as I'm cooking meat ones, I'm cooking her. Or others like her."

"Yes, but . . ." Mina didn't really know what to add. She was glad that Benny had come round to what she was saying, but she hadn't intended it all to happen so fast. She was worried that he was doing that thing he sometimes did – like when he made his speech in **Bonkers Burgers!** – of getting an idea in his head and just running with it, whatever happened. And Mina wasn't at all sure she wanted to feel responsible for this idea, given that it might lead to something very drastic for **Lenny's Burgers**. She was about to say all this when Benny grabbed her and said:

"Come on, let's go back to the van and tell my dad!"

"What? Now . . .?"

"Yes! Before he locks up!"

CHAPTER 24

But when they got back to the van, Lenny was setting off home. Benny and Mina caught up with him.

"Dad! I wanted to suggest something! About a new type of burger we should do! In fact, it should be the only burger that we do!"

"Benny . . . I think maybe you might be rushing this a bit . . ." said Mina.

"Ha ha!" said Lenny. "Don't worry, Mina. I trust

Small Fry. All his ideas have worked out so far! Let's go home and talk about it over a cup of tea!"

Father and son set off. Mina watched them, uncertainly, before heading home herself.

When they reached Bracket Wood High Street, Lenny moved to go down a back road. Benny, who was keen to have the conversation about plant burgers as soon as possible but knew it would indeed be easier at home over a cup of tea, said, "Dad. Um. Coming back from the van . . . we always go a longer way round than we need to. If we walk down the High Street, we can get home quicker . . ."

"I know, Ben."

"So . . ." said Benny, about to turn into the High Street. "Shall we . . .?"

"Um . . . I dunno."

Benny could feel the clouds of his dad's sadness forming again. He sometimes didn't like to ask what the matter was when he sensed this. But this time he said, "Dad. What's wrong?"

Lenny stopped and sighed. Then he seemed to collect himself, and said, "You're right. Let's go the quicker way."

Soon, they were passing **Bonkers Burgers!** It was full, as ever. Benny glanced over at his dad. Lenny was staring at the ground. He'd barely noticed **Bonkers Burgers!**

"Dad . . ." said Benny. "Are you OK?"

Lenny stopped. "So . . . I know you know this, Benny. But I'm not sure I've ever really explained it."

"What?"

"What this place used to be. **Kenny's**."

Benny frowned. "Yes . . . I knew it used to be here."

"Well, you were actually born here. Well, not here. You were born in hospital. But this is where me and your mum brought you back afterwards. Because we lived above **Kenny's**. You wouldn't remember, of course. But that's the thing, Benny – why I find it a bit hard to walk past here. When I lost **Kenny's**, we didn't just lose a caff. We lost our home. The one I'd lived in with your mum."

Benny looked into **Bonkers Burgers!** At the people eating and talking who didn't know this – all the people for whom it was just a place to eat burgers. Then he looked at his dad looking at them.

"Sorry, Dad."

"It's OK, son. It's good that you brought me this way. I need to get over all this eventually."

The doors opened suddenly.

"Hello, hello, hello!" said Bodley Bonkers, emerging from inside, followed by Shazad Smith, who was holding a camera. "How lovely to see you two both here!"

CHAPTER 25

"We're just making a little promotional video," said Bodley.

"OK, well done," said Lenny, not looking at him. "We'll be on our way."

"Do wait. I can't tempt you in for a free Big Bonkers or two? On the house?"

"No, thank you."

"Frightened you might like it too much?"

"I don't think so." Lenny began pulling Benny

away. But in front of them stood Michael and Michaela. Not actively stopping them. But not not stopping them either.

"Really . . ." continued Bodley. "That was just a joke. As you know . . ." And here he gestured to Shazad, who pressed a button on the camera: a red recording light came on. Bodley shifted his body slightly, still speaking to Benny and Lenny but flicking his eyes all the time towards the lens. "We were very upset about that nasty business with our ex-employee and feel that the way forward, for both **Bonkers Burgers!** and – just remind me what your van thing is called again . . ."

"**Lenny's Burgers**," said Lenny grimly.

"Right, exactly. The way forward is for us to co-exist happily – brothers in burgers, we say!"

"I wrote that," said Shazad.

"Shh," said Bodley. "So . . . I want to shake on it." He stuck his hand out. "To show we're all friends."

Lenny looked uncomfortable. So did Benny. Neither of them put their hands out.

"OK, this is awkward," said Bodley.

Still neither of them put their hands out.

"Well, I'm going to leave my hand here . . . to show my goodwill, at least. And also for another reason . . ."

"What?" said Benny, aware that this was taking a long time now.

Bodley beamed at him. "I think one way we can show our togetherness is a little competition. A fry-off."

"Fry-off?"

"Yes, I wasn't sure it should be called that. Shazad suggested it. Like bake-off. But with burgers."

"Burger-off?" said Benny.

"Hmm," said Bodley.

"Hmm," said Lenny.

"I'd stick with fry-off," Bodley said. "Anyway. Yes. An on-the-street competition. We can do it near your van if you like.

"Right . . ." said Benny.

"You cook your bestest ever burger. We cook our bestest ever burger. And the bestest of the bestest wins!"

Lenny and Benny exchanged a look, and Benny turned to Bodley.

"Wins what?"

"Oh . . . you know . . . just the . . . Oh Lord, Michael or Michaela, can you come and hold my arm up, it's starting to really hurt!"

They both lumbered over and put a hand each under Bodley's outstretched arm, thus keeping his hand out ready for the handshake, whenever it might come.

"Thank you. Yes. Well, of course the main thing wouldn't be who won or who lost. I'm just talking about a little something that we could both do to increase the profile of great burgers in the area."

"Right . . ." said Benny again. "I'm not sure burgers in general need their profile raised—"

"So," cut in Bodley. " How about we spice it up and make it more exciting with a tiny bet? Why don't we say that if we – that is, if the **Bonkers Burgers!** bestest burger is the bestest – goodness that was

hard to say! Well, if we win, then we also win . . ."
He paused and his eyes narrowed a bit. "Oh, I don't
know . . . What about, perhaps, **Kenny's Cookbook**?
And with it, the recipe for the Benny burger."

"How do you even know about that?" said Lenny
angrily.

"He came to the van, Dad!" said Benny. "In a very
bad disguise. And had a burger. You didn't notice.
But he must've seen the book on the shelf."

"HA HA HA HA HA," said Bodley, very deliberately
to the camera. "Another very good joke from Benny
B! Such a bonkers guy!" He turned back to Benny
and Lenny. "Anyway . . . Michael and Michaela can't
hold my arm up forever. What say you?"

Benny and Lenny exchanged another look. Then
Benny frowned and glared at Bodley. "And what if
we win?"

Bodley looked confused. "Pardon?"

"What if we win? What do we win? If my burger

is the . . . bestest?"

Bodley looked at Shazad, who just shrugged.

"Hmm. I hadn't even thought of that. Is that how these things work then?"

"Bets?" said Benny. "Yep." He thought for a second, then looked to his father again, and finally said to Bodley, "OK. If you win – you win the cookbook. With the secret recipe in there for the Benny burger. But if we win . . ."

"Yes?" said Bodley impatiently. Then to Lenny: "Is he always this long-winded?"

"We win . . . this," said Benny.

Bodley frowned. "What?"

"This."

"This what? Bit of pavement?"

"No," said Benny. He raised a hand and pointed to **Bonkers Burgers!** "These premises."

Bodley's eyes boggled. "WHAT? YOU WIN **BONKERS BURGERS!**?"

"Not the whole company, obviously. Just this branch."

Benny peeked sideways at his dad. He was smiling. He looked like he couldn't believe what his son was saying. But he was smiling.

"HA HA HA HA HA HA HA!" said Bodley, though he was not smiling.

Benny stuck his hand out, grasped Bodley's hand and shook it.

"Not a joke," he said.

CHAPTER 26

"Are you sure about this, Small Fry?" said Lenny, not for the first time.

"No," replied Benny.

"Right. So shall we call off the fry-off? It's in six days – I think that's enough time to cancel it and—"

"No," said Benny.

"Explain?" Lenny finished.

Benny looked his dad in the eye. "I know you're

my dad and the older one, so you're supposed to pass on wise advice to me – rather than the other way round – but one thing I've heard is people saying that if you had to be sure about everything before you did it, you'd never do anything."

"Yes. You're right." Lenny took a deep breath. "Listen, I've got faith in you, son."

Yes! So have we all," Mina added. She was with them in their living room, along with Jasper, after Lenny had called a meeting of "all concerned" about the upcoming Fry-Off. Mina turned to Jasper and said, "Haven't we, Jasper?"

"Oh, yeah," replied Jasper. "Definitely."

Benny looked at him.

"What?" said Jasper. "Is it my fault my voice just sounds sarcastic?"

There was a ping on Lenny's phone.

"Oh," he said, as he checked the notification. "Who's René von Rathsack?"

Benny frowned. "He's the head chef at Smørgöswispa."

"Pardon?" said everyone.

"Shmor-gosh-visper," said Benny. "It's the most famous restaurant in the world. It's got seventeen Sanitaire medals."

"OMG!" said Jasper. "Or at least that's what I might say if I knew what those were."

"They're awards for posh food," said Benny. "Usually even the poshest restaurants only have about two or three."

"Sanitaire?" said Mina.

"They're the sponsors of the awards," Benny explained. "They make toilets. Posh ones."

Mina nodded. "Right."

"Anyway, Dad. What about him?"

"Um . . ." Lenny showed them his phone. There was a news article on the screen, with the headline:

WORLD'S GREATEST CHEF TO CREATE NEW BURGER FOR BONKERS

And underneath Benny read out: "René von Rathsack, head chef of Smørgöswispa, to design 'most delicious gourmet burger ever' for crazy fast-food chain."

"Oh," said Mina.

"Yes . . ." said Lenny.

Benny frowned. "Do you think that's got anything to do with our fry-off? I mean . . . does this mean . . . the fry-off is going to be me versus the greatest chef in the world?"

The others didn't say anything. Lenny looked

down. Mina shut her eyes. Jasper started whistling.

Eventually Lenny spoke, though less confidently than before: "I've got faith in you, son."

CHAPTER 27

"Thanks, Dad," said Benny, still staring at the headline on his dad's phone. "Ow!"

"What?" said Lenny.

But it was Mina. She had nudged her friend in the side.

"That hurt!" he said.

"I'm just trying to get you to remember something," she said.

Benny frowned.

She raised her eyebrows as high as they would go, but Benny just stared at her. Eventually she went: "Moooooooooo!"

There was a pause.

"Is everything all right, Mina?" said Lenny.

"Baaaa?" said Jasper.

Benny blinked. "Yes! Sorry," he said, then he turned to Lenny. "Ah . . . Dad, here's the thing." He wondered how to say it: whether to build up to it, or pad around it, or say some things that might lead his dad to guess what he meant. Instead he came out with:

"IvedecidedImgoingtocookjustveganburgersfrom nowon."

"Sorry?" said Lenny.

"Yes. Sorry?" echoed Jasper.

"Say it slower, Benny," said Mina patiently.

Benny took a deep breath. "I've decided, um, that I'm going . . . to cook just vegan burgers from now on."

Lenny stared at him. Jasper stared at him even harder.

"Why?" said Lenny.

"Um . . . well . . ." said Benny. "Mina took me to see Dottie."

"And what did Dottie say to you?" asked Lenny.

"Um . . ."

"Moooooooo," went Mina again.

Lenny looked at her. "I take it Dottie is a cow."

"At the Bracket Wood City Farm," Mina said, nodding.

"Yes, well," said Benny. "I liked Dottie. Meeting her was a bit like meeting . . . a person. Like you and me and Mina and Jasper."

"Not me," said Jasper. "I'm really nothing like a cow."

Benny took another deep breath. "OK, but anyway . . . that's what I realised when I went to the city farm. And so I promised Mina that from now on I would only cook non-meat burgers."

Lenny and Jasper stared at Mina.

"I . . . yes. I did tell him he should think about it for a bit," said Mina. "Not decide that right away. But . . . well . . . You know what Benny's like . . ."

Lenny nodded. "I'm his dad."

"Yes."

"OK," said Jasper. "You made a stupid promise. We've all done that. What you need to do now,

Benny, is . . . break it."

Benny thought for a second. Then he shook his head. "A promise is a promise," he said. "Now that is something you've always told me, Dad."

"Have I? Oh dear," said Lenny.

"Look!" said Benny. "It's going to be fine. As Mina always says, there are plant burgers now that are impossible to tell apart from meat ones."

"Yes, of course," said Jasper.

"Is that just your voice again, or are you actually being sarcastic now?" said Mina.

"And I can do it!" continued Benny. "I will do my best against the best chef in the world! And I can cook a plant burger that will taste just as good as my meat burger! I can win the fry-off! All I need is the support of the people around me!" He looked at each of them in turn. "You guys!"

"Right!" said Mina. "You've got it, Benny!"

"Yes, good with luck with that!" said Jasper.

"That's definitely not just your voice now, is it? That's what people say when they're being sarcastic," said Benny, to which Jasper smiled and gave a shrug. Benny sighed and turned to Lenny. "Anyway, Dad?"

There was a long, long pause. Then Lenny looked at Benny, nodded, and said:

"I've got faith in—"

He was going to say "you, son" – he definitely was – but unfortunately he started coughing a lot and never quite managed it.

CHAPTER 28

"Oh dear," said Benny, putting the burger down.

"I think it's OK," said Mina, chewing. She was, however, chewing with some difficulty.

"What did you say?" said Jasper.

Mina swallowed hard. "I said, I think it's OK."

"Oh. Because it sounded like you were saying, Mbghbghd blergh glhupp drrup. Almost as if you had some horrible gloop in your mouth or something."

"You're really not helping, Jasper," she said.

194

"No, but he's right," said Benny. "This first food test is going down as –" he wrote on a little pad next to the plate – "two out of ten."

"Generous," said Jasper.

They were in the van. It was not, though, a Saturday. Lenny had opened the van for Benny to practise grilling: or, to be more precise, to practise his technique on a new type of burger. Mina had provided the patties, which she had bought from a shop near her house that sold vegan food. Benny had cooked a few, and they'd built the burgers as they always did. But each patty had felt wrong even when they were still on the grill. He couldn't get exactly the right delicious blackened crust. He tried cooking them for longer, but then they just went dry inside. As he pressed down with his spatula, he didn't get that slow rebound he normally got that made him know that the texture would be soft and juicy inside. Even the sound of the sizzle was wrong.

The one they were trying now was the fifth attempt.

"Is it the patties?" said Benny. "Maybe we should try different ones?"

"I don't understand," said Mina. "These ones are usually really good."

"I heard . . ." said Jasper, " . . . that in some countries they're actually growing meat now, in laboratories. From animal cells."

"Oh right, yes," Mina said. "Well, Jasper, why don't we get on a plane to those countries then, and see if they'll lend some of their space meat to three kids . . .?"

"Is that your sarcastic voice now?" Jasper retorted.

"What are we going to do?" said Benny.

Mina looked away from Jasper. She frowned. "Maybe we need to change your recipe . . . to fit the new burger?"

Benny considered this. "But . . . I want it to taste exactly like a Benny burger. That was the point."

"Hello, all . . ." said Lenny, entering the van. "How's it going?"

"Yes! Great, Dad!" said Benny, sounding not at all convincing.

"Oh. Good." Lenny picked up the half-eaten burger, still on the plate.

"No!" said Benny.

"Eh?"

"It's . . . gone cold."

Lenny moved it towards his mouth. "Well, OK, I can still taste whether it's good or not—"

"No! I've already taken a big bite out of it."

"I can see that," said Lenny, "but I don't care."

It was nearly at his lips.

"I WEED ON IT!" shouted Benny.

Lenny froze. "Pardon?"

"I . . . weed on it," said Benny.

Mina stared at him, shaking her head.

Lenny frowned. "Is that part of a new recipe?"

"Benny's lying, Mr Burns," said Mina. "He's lying because we can't quite get the burger to taste right. So he didn't want you to taste it."

"Oh. Well. That isn't great news. But better news than you weeing on it to try and make it taste better, I suppose." Lenny glanced from Benny to Mina. "Oh, by the way, I read in the local paper that something was going on with that city farm that you two like."

"Something?" said Mina.

"Bad, I'm afraid."

CHAPTER 29

"Moooo . . ." said Dottie, seeing Mina.

But this time Mina didn't moo back. Her eyes were red, and her face was sad.

"I can't believe it," she said.

"Neither can I," said Benny. "Does the whole place have to be sold?"

"I'm as sad as you are," said Baku, who was standing next to them. "But the money situation is worse than I realised. We're bankrupt, basically."

Benny hesitated. Then he said, "So what's going to happen to Dottie? And the others?"

Baku sighed and shrugged. "We'll try and find some other farm to place her. Otherwise . . ."

She didn't finish that sentence, but Benny and Mina knew what she meant.

There was a long period of silence, broken by the occasional plaintive moo from Dottie, who seemed to understand that something was wrong.

"Who's buying it?" said Benny eventually.

CHAPTER 30

"Well, that's **Bonkers Burgers!** for you," said Lenny, after Benny and Mina had come back to the van and shared the news about the Bracket Wood City Farm. "That's exactly what they did with **Kenny's**. They go looking for a place that's in trouble, then offer a tiny amount to buy it – the poor seller's got no choice, so they have to accept!"

"That's terrible," said Mina.

"No, it's not," said Jasper. "It's just business."

"Well, whatever it is, I can tell you one thing," said Benny. "It means we definitely have to win the fry-off now. We've got to teach **Bonkers Burgers!** a lesson!"

Everyone agreed. But then they all glanced at the plant burger, still cold and uneaten on a plate next to the grill.

"Hmm . . ." said Lenny.

"Hmm is right," said Jasper. "It's humming."

"Benny," said Mina. "You know what I said earlier about maybe changing the recipe of the Benny burger, to suit a plant one . . .?"

"Mina," said Benny, starting to sound cross — which he never usually did with Mina. But, all in all, he was beginning to feel very under pressure. "I said already I'm not doing that."

"OK," said Mina gently, "but maybe just go back and look at the original recipe in the cookbook.

Maybe there's something in there that you hadn't noticed . . . that might help . . ."

"Um . . ." said Benny, even crosser this time, "I've read my grandad's cookbook, like, from cover to cover."

"Mina," said Jasper. "Why did you force Benny to make a promise about only cooking vegan burgers! That was like . . . the worst thing you could've done right now!"

Mina stared at him. "I didn't force Benny to do anything! I just took him to the city farm, and talked to him about what things are like for animals. I never expected him to stop cooking meat altogether. That was Benny's decision. Benny . . . That's true, isn't it?"

Benny looked at her. He knew it was indeed true, but he was also feeling overwhelmed with the challenge of winning the competition, and the cost of losing, for him, and for his dad. He thought about going back on his promise not to cook meat burgers any more, but then he remembered Dottie and the other animals in danger at City Farm – no, he couldn't break that promise. A part of him blamed Mina for putting him in this position, even though another part of him knew it wasn't her fault at all. And so . . . he didn't say anything. He just looked away.

He heard a sob and a door slamming. When he looked up, Mina had gone.

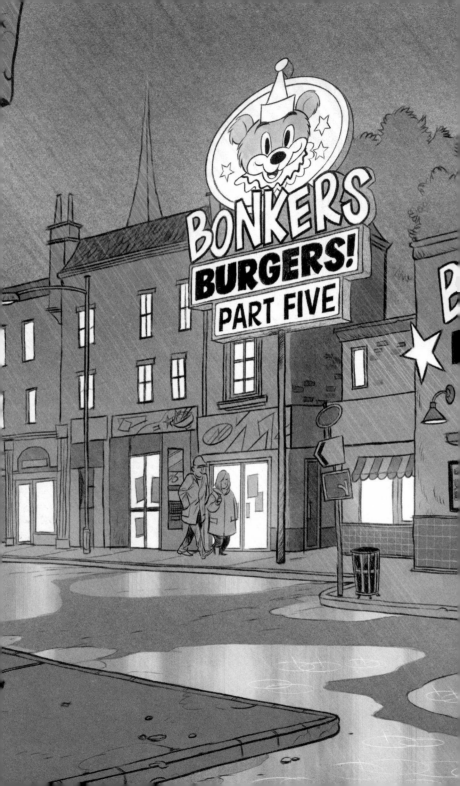

CHAPTER 31

The day of the fry-off had come. And with it, this announcement on both flyers and social media:

Benny read this, and, for the first time, noticed an obvious problem with the whole idea.

"But who's going to be judging it?" he said.

Lenny shrugged. "Maybe we just pass the burgers round for everyone to try and then there'll be a show of hands?"

"Yes," said Jasper, "because **Bonkers Burgers!** have shown themselves to be the height of fairness so far, haven't they?"

"Your voice really does sound sarcastic, doesn't it?" said Lenny.

"What should we do?" asked Benny. "We should have thought of this before, shouldn't we? When we took the bet." He looked again at the announcement. "Because it's today."

"Yes. Well, it's too late to pull out," Lenny replied. "We'll look like cowards. We'll just have to try and keep an eye on any shenanigans the Bonkers lot pull when it comes to judging. In fact, I'm going to go out now and ask around to see if anyone knows what they might be planning . . ."

Benny nodded, and watched as his dad and Jasper left the van. He was dressed in his chef's whites. They didn't look that bright, because he was sitting in semi-darkness. He was feeling incredibly nervous. After the argument with Mina, he had pretended for a while that nothing was wrong, but further attempts to make a Benny burger using vegan patties had not improved matters.

Nothing he made tasted quite right. He was sure he was going to lose the fry-off.

In desperation, he picked up his dad's phone and wrote to the one person who he hoped might help.

Dear Juliana Skeffington . . .

It's Benny Burns here (you very kindly wrote to me once

before). I have to do a sort of cooking competition today. This one.

I'm a bit nervous. I won't bore you with all the details, but I can't seem to get the taste right like I used to. Any advice appreciated. Thank you so much, Benny.

He posted the message using his dad's social media account, replying to the one she'd sent to him.

He waited in the dark for a while. But nothing happened. He hadn't expected it to. She was a very busy woman who got hundreds of messages a day.

Benny sighed and stretched his arms. As he did so, **Kenny's Cookbook** caught his eye; it was just about visible in the dim light. He remembered Mina's words. He grabbed the book and opened

212

it. He used the torch on his dad's phone to illuminate the page he needed – the first one, which had the heading "The Secret Ingredient". He stared at it for a minute, as if somehow just looking at it might help.

Suddenly light flooded into the van.

"Benny!" said Lenny. "Come on! They're here!"

Outside, the sun was bright and the sky was blue. The crowd had grown. From where he was standing in front of the van, Benny looked around and saw Bodley Bonkers, Michael and Michaela – and the rest of them. They were all wearing **Bonkers Burgers!**

hats and **Bonkers Burgers!** badges and waving **Bonkers Burgers!** flags. One or two were dressed in full Bonkers bear outfits. Behind them was a large black car with blacked-out windows. Set up next to it was an enormous portable cooking station. It was glossy and huge, made of the shiniest stainless steel. On one side was a chopping board the size of the burger van's counter, and on the other side, very neatly stacked, were piles of – also extremely shiny – pans and saucepans and ladles and knives.

A tall man came out of the car. Like Benny, he was wearing chef's whites, but his looked much more expensive. Over them he wore a black apron, which had embroidered on it in white: *Smörgöswispa*. The man walked slowly to the cooking station. He bent down to the level of the steel surfaces, his eyes coming down close to the grill, hobs and switches, looking for a moment more like a snooker player than a chef. He seemed, to Benny, to be delicately smelling his outdoor kitchen.

"Yesh," he said. "It ish good." He spoke perfect English with a strong foreign accent, though his S's came out as "sh". "Chef ish pleashed."

"Chef?" said Bodley Bonkers, coming over.

"Yesh. I am Chef."

"Right. Of course." Bodley frowned. "Sorry, I thought your name was René von Rathsack?"

"When I am in a kitchen, my name ish Chef. Unless you think thish ish not a kitchen. In which case, you may call me René. But if you think thish ish not a real kitchen, vot are ve doing here?"

"Right. Yes. Of course," said Bodley. "It's the most proper outdoor kitchen money can buy . . . Chef."

"Team René!" said the famous chef, clicking his fingers. Immediately, three people wearing chef's whites and similar aprons got out of the car. They grouped around René von Rathsack, seeming to bend a bit, as if bowing towards him. "My shalad chef. My bread chef. My shous-chef," he announced.

Bodley nodded. "Don't they have names?"

"Here they are also just called Chef. But in their case: Shalad Chef, Bread Chef and Shous—"

"OK, yes I get it."

"What's a sous-chef?" said Milly Mackay slightly nervously.

"The shecond-in-command in the kitchen," said René, putting his arm round the still-apparently-bowing young woman who was his sous-chef. "My right-hand pershon. A very important job."

"And," said Millie more nervously, "you need all these to cook a burger?"

Everyone fell silent. Everyone looked at René.

"Sho . . ." said René, "you think a burger is not real food?"

"Well, I do work for Bonkers Burg— um, no, of coursh – I mean, of course not," said Milly.

"Food," said René, "any food, can be great food. You think high cuisine is just shnails?"

"Pardon?"

"Shnails?"

"Oh, snails."

"Or côte de boeuf? Or turbot, cooked in itsh own

217

juishes, with a glaze of pomegranate and shcallops? I mean, obvioushly, I can make those dishes. Many, many timesh. And people have shaid, Yesh, Chef, thish ish the highest, mosht beautiful cuisine anyone can ever make! Of coursh they have. But you think I cannot bring the shame shkill, the shame preshishon—"

"Pardon?"

"Preshishon."

"Precision, right," said Milly.

"And," René continued, gesturing to the others, "the shame team to the lowlier foods? To chips. To shaushages. To –" and here his sous-chef produced a silver plate, on which was some very red, very juicy, very expensive-looking and undeniably meaty mince meat – "burgersh?"

"I agree," said a voice. It was Benny's.

CHAPTER 32

"Well, thank you, young man," said René, walking round the cooking station to stand in front of Benny, who had to look up a long way to meet the famous chef's gaze. "Good to have your shupport."

"Yes. Well," said Benny. "I just mean that I agree that any food – not just posh food – can be made to taste really nice. If you cook it with lov—"

"With shkill and preshishon, as I said," interrupted René. "Exactly."

"Well, I was going to say, with . . ."

"And I love what you're wearing, little fellow. The chef's whites! Have you come dresshed like this because you are a fan of mine? Perhaps you follow me on the internet? I know you won't ever have been able to afford to come to any of my reshtaurants, but you can shee pictures and dream from afar, can't you? Hey, maybe today I will let you try a tiny bit of the amazing burger that I will be making. How fabuloush is that?"

"Um . . ." said Bodley Bonkers, inserting himself between René and Benny. "This boy is . . . not just a fan. This is Benny. He's your rival today. He's the other cook. In the fry-off."

René looked at Bodley, then at Benny, and again at Bodley

"HA HA HA HA HA HA!" said René.

"HA HA HA HA HA HA!" said Bodley, although he looked a bit confused to be doing his laughing thing when he hadn't told a joke.

"That ish very funny! That ish a good one! Your British sense of humour! Although I thought you were American?"

"HA HA HA HA . . . Actually, no," said Bodley, suddenly stopping the laughter. "He really is. The other chef."

René frowned. He looked down at Benny.

"Hi," said Benny.

"Exschuse me a moment," said René. He moved about ten metres away, gesturing for Bodley to follow. His team of chefs watched, looking terrified. René bent down, so that his face was very close to Bodley's.

"You sheem," said René, loud enough for Lenny and Benny to hear, even though he had presumably moved away so that they couldn't, "to have mishunderstood who I am. I am the winner of eighteen Sanitaire medals—"

"I thought it was sheventeen – sorry, seventeen," said Bodley.

"I have a new one. As of last week. It's a lot of medalsh. Not that I make a fussh of it. But basically I am the besht shef in the shtratosphere."

"Pardon?"

"In the world. I am René von Rathsack. And you want me to cook against –" René turned to glare at Benny – "an eleven-year-old who worksh . . . in a burger van?"

"Well," said Shazad Smith, coming forward to join the huddle. He held up a piece of paper. "It was in your contract, René."

"Wash it . . ."

"No, you can't do that to paper. It would go all soggy."

"I don't read contractsh," said René. "Too boring."

"OK," said Bodley. "Got it. You're a genius. Of course. But if you were to check this one, you'd see we are paying you exactly . . ." At this point, Benny couldn't hear what he whispered, as Bodley tiptoed up so that his mouth was close to René's ear.

Bodley stood back down, and René looked at him. He tilted his head to one side thoughtfully. Then he strode quickly over to Benny and bent down, sticking his hand out.

"Benny, may the besht chef win!"

CHAPTER 33

During this time, the crowd had got bigger. There were murmurs and some applause as the two chefs took their positions: René von Rathsack behind the gleaming outdoor cooking station, and Benny Burns standing on a chair at the grill in his dad's van.

A small stage had been set up between the two teams. Bodley Bonkers walked up the steps on to it and looked out at the crowd. "Hello and welcome to the Bracket Wood Bonkers Fry-off, sponsored by

Bonkers Burgers!" He paused, clearly awaiting an excited audience reaction. None came. He looked round at his Top Brass, frowning and sticking his palms out.

"Oh!" said Shazad Smith, and he started applauding frantically. All the other employees did the same. Eventually the crowd joined in, confused.

"Thank you," said Bodley. "So, the competition will last twenty minutes. One patty will be cooked by both chefs, to the best of their abilities. It will be placed in a bread roll, and then, with the addition of salad and sauce, made into the thing we all love: a burger!"

He paused again. Shazad applauded madly, along with the rest of the **Bonkers Burgers!** team, but this time nobody else copied them.

"And then that burger," Bodley continued, "will be judged on its looks and, more importantly, its taste. So, burger chefs . . . three, two—"

"Who's judging it?"

Bodley looked round, surprised at the interruption. It was Edith, at the front of the crowd.

"Who's the judge?" she shouted. "Of the burgers?"

"Oh," said Bodley. "Me."

A murmur rippled through the crowd.

"That's not fair," said Edith.

"HA HA HA HA HA!" said Bodley.

"And not funny," she added.

Bodley frowned. "I think you're forgetting, madam, that **Bonkers Burgers!** – the company I own and run – sponsored this fry-off. So, I will decide who the judge is. Thank you very much."

"Excuse me," said Lenny, glancing at Benny. "We thought something like this might be the case. But I think if you're going to be a judge, then I should be the second judge."

Bodley stared at him. "Are you suggesting that I might be biased?"

Lenny stared back. "Yes."

"How dare you."

"Well, if you're not, you'll let me be a judge."

"But you're obviously biased."

"Sir . . ." said Sarah Sherbet uncertainly. "Maybe we should pick someone out of the crowd to be the third judge? You know . . . the casting vote?"

"I'm OK with that!" said Lenny, as a few people in the crowd applauded that suggestion.

"I don't know," said Bodley.

"It'll be fine," said Sarah Sherbet.

"Will it?"

"Yes, sir," said Sarah Sherbet emphatically. "It will."

"Oh! I see," said Bodley. "I get it."

"Hello? Chef here? Waiting to shtart this shtupid competition?" shouted René.

"No problem!" said Bodley. "So, let's start again. Burger chefs – three, two, one, FRY!"

*

Within five minutes, René's salad chef, bread chef and sous-chef were working away. The salad chef was chopping lettuce and tomatoes and onions. The bread chef was cradling a sesame-seed bun. The sous-chef held out a tiny glass bowl. René nodded, then very delicately took a pinch of salt from it – *Kosher?* wondered Benny, watching nervously – and sprinkled it on Team René's expensive-looking meat patty.

Benny looked round. His dad was struggling into his greasy apron. Jasper was opening the fridge and getting out meat patties, pointedly ignoring the one vegan patty that Benny had already placed on a plate covered with cling film on the top shelf. Benny's eyes scanned the shelves. They were empty of ingredients.

He looked out at Team René – another tiny bowl had been placed in front of René, containing what looked like pepper, but René was refusing it, demanding another bowl with, Benny assumed, posher pepper. Benny sighed. Maybe they should just give up now, he thought.

He looked at the crowd. Some of them, the ones interested in cooking, were watching intently. Others, the ones who weren't, had started talking to each other. He felt dead inside. He should have been so much more excited, but he just knew they were going to lose.

"Chefs! You have fifteen minutes left!" shouted Bodley Bonkers, who was now back on the stage.

"Can you bring me the patty?" said Benny, his voice flat as he stood at the counter. "And don't muck about, Jasper. Just bring me the right one."

"This one?" said a voice behind him.

He turned round. It was Mina. She was wearing a white apron. And holding out a plate with something that looked like blobs of mince on it.

"Oh!" said Benny, incredibly pleased. "You came back!"

She smiled. "I thought you might need a sous-chef."

CHAPTER 34

"I'm sorry, so sorry," said Benny. "I should've said something before – when Jasper was being horrible about you – I knew I should have done – but I was so worried about this competition and everything . . . But I took your advice. I went to look at the cookbook again – at

the recipe and the secret ingredient . . . and I think maybe now I understand that—"

"Can you shut up, please," said Mina, "and start cooking?"

"Right you are," said Benny. "But . . . what is this?"

"It's plant mince. I know you were having trouble making the burgers as good as they used to be. So I thought you should make the patty yourself, rather than me buying it already made."

Benny stared at her. "Oh, of course! Why didn't I think of that?"

"I don't know. Maybe because you don't quite trust yourself with vegan food yet? But you can trust me. And . . ." she looked at him, deep into his eyes, "I believe in you, Benny."

"Really?"

"Yes," she said.

"So do I!" said Lenny.

"And me," said Jasper.

"You don't even sound sarcastic," said Benny, amazed.

Jasper grinned. "I know. It was quite hard."

Benny looked at the plate covered with tiny balls of non-meat. Then, without really thinking too much about it, he started kneading the plant mince together, massaging and moulding it into a ball. It seemed to grow redder and richer as his fingers pressed deeper into it. He dug his fingers into a bag of flour, which his dad had placed on the counter, adding a pinch to the mix. Then he spread the ball on the chopping board in front of him. From his apron, he took out a round metal cutter, and pressed down on the flattened mix. His hand rested there for a second, then carefully he lifted it. He brushed away the excess mince at the edges, and there it was: a perfectly round non-meat patty.

"Sous-chef . . ." he said, his voice suddenly confident. "We need some salt. And pepper. A clove of garlic. Mixed herbs. A tiny bit of chilli. Do we have all those things?"

She bent down and picked up a carrier bag. "I went to the supermarket on the way here, just in case. I kind of guessed what you might want," she said as she took out everything he'd just asked for, one by one.

Benny looked at her with gratitude. "Thank you," he said.

"Enough with the thanks and the sorrys," said Mina with a smile. "Get chopping!"

Jasper came forward and handed Benny a knife. With skill and speed much greater than his years, Benny peeled a clove of garlic and began chopping it into extra-thin white slivers. Then, he threw a careful amount of herbs and chilli into the plant mince.

Next, Benny turned to the grill, which Lenny had turned on the moment the contest had started.

Benny poured on some oil, and sprinkled the salt on it, followed by the garlic.

He lost all the fear and uncertainty that had been coming off him like a bad smell only minutes earlier. Benny was In The Zone, almost like a dancer, seeming to know instinctively where to move and what to crush and how to mould: as if he could cook blindfolded.

He slid a spatula underneath the patty and placed it on the hot black metal of the grill. What followed was a sound that everyone in the van had been waiting for: a sizzle.

"OK," said Benny. "Now the sauce."

Mina and Jasper were ready. From the fridge, Jasper produced tomato ketchup, mayonnaise, lemon juice, mustard and vinegar. Without any need for precise measuring, Benny put splodges and drops of each in a bowl, and then whirled the mixture around with a fork. Mina opened a jar of sweet-and-sour pickles, and laid one out on to the chopping board. Benny sliced the pickle into tiny pieces, then added them to the sauce mixture.

Without missing a beat, he turned back to the patty, flipping it once with the spatula. Then back over again. Then back once more. He pressed with the spatula on the patty's surface. It sizzled, again. The sizzle – there it was. The sound of perfection.

"What are you doing?" said Jasper.

"Trying to get a nice crust," Benny replied. "I never did that before because I didn't think I could get the right texture on a non-meat patty. But a burger should be crunchy on the outside and moist on the inside. And I think I can get there now . . ."

He continued to flip it, in time with some secret music he seemed to hear in his head. A wonderful aroma began to fill the van. Benny's instinct told him: Now's the time.

236

"Dad. Split a bun."

Lenny quickly opened a sesame bun and handed the two halves to Benny, who placed them on the grill, close to the patty.

"It's good for the buns to pick up some flavour from the cooking," he said.

"As ever, Small Fry," said Lenny.

"Mina. Cheese."

She was ready, next to Benny, holding a plate on which were ten slices of vegan cheese. Benny lifted each one, his eyes assessing them like a professional tennis player looking through balls handed to him by a ball person. He chose a slice from the middle and laid it carefully on the patty.

"It has to melt on to the patty," he said, "but just at the corners."

"We know!" said Jasper, Lenny and Mina together.

That was the last anyone said for a while. Silence fell in the van, apart from the sizzle of the patty.

Benny was too absorbed in his cooking to even look up, but Lenny could see that, across from them, René had finished cooking his patty. He'd placed it on a plate on the side, and was poking a small glass stick into it.

"We let the meat resht now for a few minutes," he was saying, "until the thermometer shows the optimum temperature, which, ash we know, is shixty degressh Shelsiush."

"Pardon, chef?" said his sous-chef.

"Shixty-degressh shelsiush."

"Yep," said the sous-chef. "Actually, no. Sorry. Once more?"

"What is the matter with you guysh?! One hundred and forty in Fahrenheit!"

"Right! Got it!"

In the van, Lenny gulped. "Um . . . should we be doing that?"

"Well," said Benny, "I'll let our non-meat rest too."

"But we haven't got a meat thermometer."

"I could go and get my parents' one," said Jasper.

"Yes, but that's not a cooking thermometer. It's been up your—"

"It's fine," said Benny, sliding the spatula underneath the patty, covered beautifully in the just-melted cheese, and placing it on a plate, held by Mina. "I'll feel it."

"With your hands?" said Lenny.

"No, I'll just know how long to rest it for. Salad ingredients, please!"

A lettuce, a tomato and an onion were quickly presented to him. Again, he looked with precise eyes at each. He tore the lettuce apart, smelling it for freshness. He found the perfect leaves and set them aside. Expertly, he sliced the tomato and onion, choosing the best sections. Mina got a pickle from the jar, as before, and Benny sliced it finely, arranging the slices into small circles.

Finally, he picked up the sliced bun, lightly toasted, and placed the halves, grilled side up, on a plate in front of him. He took the sauce from the bowl and spread a perfect amount of it on each half. On one side, he carefully arranged the lettuce, tomato, onion and pickle, the lettuce going first, so the rest of the salad rested in its green embrace. Finally, he looked at the patty, paused for a couple of seconds, then with the spatula lifted it and slid it gracefully on to the other half of the bun. It rested there, like something full of potential, waiting for its moment.

"And now," Benny said, "the moment of truth."

Mina, Jasper and Lenny watched with bated breath as he picked up the two halves and squashed them together. Loaded as they were, they seemed to fit like two things that had always been made for each other.

Benny placed the combined halves on the plate.

He held the plate up, looking at it for a moment.

And then he looked at the others and said:

"Well. It's a Benny burger."

CHAPTER 35

Both burgers were cooked and ready. Both chefs stood behind the plates on which the burgers sat. The crowd, which had grown to quite a size, were rumbling with excitement. Their stomachs were also rumbling, due to the delicious smells coming from both kitchens. Bodley Bonkers walked up the little steps of the little stage.

"Right!" he said, addressing the crowd. "It's Judgement Day! Or . . . Judgement Time, I suppose.

Because it's not going to take the whole day. Um, anyway . . . It's time to judge the burgers is what I mean."

There was a ripple of confused applause.

"Mr Lenny,'" said Bodley. "If you would come over to the **Bonkers Burgers!**-sponsored kitchen to taste the burger cooked by the legendary René von Rathsack, please!"

Lenny wiped his hands on his apron, thus making it more greasy and marked, and walked from the van to René's still-sparkling outdoor kitchen.

René smiled at him.

"Enjoy," he said.

"It looks amazing," said Lenny.

René shrugged, with an air of "everything I cook ish amazing". Then, with great expertise, he sliced the burger he had cooked into three. He put a third each on two plates and offered them to Lenny and Bodley. They bit into their bits.

"OMG," said Lenny.

"Goodness," said Bodley.

"Yesh," said René smugly.
"I know."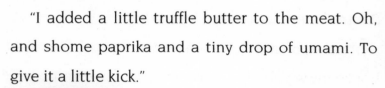

"How have you got that tashte – sorry, that taste?" said Lenny.

"I added a little truffle butter to the meat. Oh, and shome paprika and a tiny drop of umami. To give it a little kick."

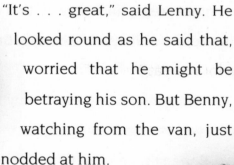"It's . . . great," said Lenny. He looked round as he said that, worried that he might be betraying his son. But Benny, watching from the van, just nodded at him.

"It is great," said Bodley, munching through the rest of it. He turned to the crowd, and announced: "And we will be offering it at Bonkers Burgers!

as our new special: the Gourmet Bonkers Big One!"

"Er. . . excushe me?"

"We will be offering it—"

"No need to shout," said René. "Have we agreed that?"

"Yes, it's also in your contract," shouted Shazad Smith.

René sighed. "We really have to call it the Gourmet Bonkers Big One?"

"Look, we can discuss all this later," said Bodley. "Meanwhile, Benny of **Lenny's Burgers** has, I think, a lot to beat!"

With that, Bodley and Lenny turned and walked towards the van.

CHAPTER 36

"Have we got two clean plates, Mina?" Benny said quickly.

"On it!" she said, and arrived with them just before Bodley and Lenny got to the van's serving window.

"Here you go, gentlemen," said Benny.

"Hmm . . ." said Bodley. "I don't know if the look of this one is quite up to René's . . ."

"I think it looks great!" said Lenny, although

without that much conviction.

"It probably doesn't look as good," said Benny, "but I believe the proof of the pudding is in the eating."

Bodley frowned. "It's not a pudding though."

"It's an idiom," said Lenny.

"How dare you!"

"Idiom. Like a saying."

"Please, don't let it get too cold," said Benny.

Lenny and Bodley picked up their thirds, and bit into them.

"Oh, that's good. So good," said Lenny. "And this patty is actually—"

"Shh," said Benny. "Don't want to give that away . . ."

But he needn't have worried. Because, as with his first Benny burger, Bodley Bonkers was lost. He was lost in a taste wonderland. It seemed that all he was, was his tongue. He bit into the burger again and

the world seemed to exist in slow motion, as if just by eating it, the moment might never end.

"Bodley...?" said Lenny.

"Hmm?"

"What's your verdict?"

"Um . . ." Bodley shook himself out of his taste trance. "Yeah. It's fine."

"Fine?"

"Yeah. A good seven out of ten. Very good. For a boy and all that."

Benny looked disappointed, but he held himself together, saying, "Thank you. Shall I take your plate away?"

"Yes," replied Bodley, but not before he'd quickly eaten his last morsel of burger.

"OK!" said Bodley, turning to the crowd. "Now the time has come to reveal who we, the judges, think should be the winners of the Bracket Wood Bonkers Fry-off, sponsored by **Bonkers Burgers!**"

"Do you have to say the whole title every time?" said Lenny.

"Yes, I have to say the Bracket Wood Bonkers Fry-off, sponsored by **Bonkers Burgers!**"

"You can't just call it the Fry-Off? The competition?"

"No, I have to say the—"

"Please don't say it again."

"Well, I've started now."

"No, you didn't actually say the first word."

"The first word is the . . ." he said, and then very quickly: "BracketWoodBonkersFryOffSponsoredBy **BonkersBurgers!** winner announcement time!"

CHAPTER 37

Back on the little stage, Bodley stood with Lenny. René von Rathsack and Benny were at their cooking stations, waiting for their judgement.

"Right, Mr Lenny Burns. Whose burger would you say was the best? René or Benny's?"

"Well . . . obviously one of the chefs is my son. And Mr von Rathsack's burger was very nice indeed. A little rich for me, perhaps."

A snorting sound was heard. It was René von Rathsack.

"Are you OK, chef?" said one of his team.

"Yesh. I wash shnorting. In dishgusht."

"But, as I say, Mr von Rathsack's was very, very good," continued Lenny hurriedly. "The thing is, I just felt that Benny's burger had a—"

Bodley rolled his eyes. "Yes, yes. We don't need an essay. You vote for Benny. Yes?"

"I do, yes. I honestly preferred it."

"OK. One vote for Benny and **Lenny's Burgers**. And I vote for . . ."

Bodley paused. Everyone looked at him. He continued to pause. Everyone continued to look at him.

"Er . . . yes?" said Lenny eventually.

"It's a dramatic pause. Like on talent shows."

"Oh. OK."

Bodley continued to pause.

"Are you still pausing?" said Lenny.

"Well, yes," huffed Bodley. "You ruined the last one. So I've started again."

"On telly shows," shouted Jasper from the van, "they have lights and music that goes da-doom, da-doom, da-doom during the pauses. They don't work otherwise."

"Is that right . . ." said Bodley, pretending he knew that all along. "OH HA HA HA—"

"Actually it is right, sir, I think," said Sarah Sherbet quietly.

"Is it? Oh, OK," said Bodley. "I vote for the René von Rathsack Gourmet Bonkers Big One!"

"Ish it already called that?" shouted René with some anguish.

"Contractually, yes," said Shazad Smith.

"I vote for it because I think it is the best burger," continued Bodley, "and not just because I am the CEO of **Bonkers Burgers!** That is nothing to do with my decision!"

"Right," said Jasper loudly.

"It's true! There's no need for the sarcasm, young man!" said Bodley.

"His voice always sounds like that," said Lenny.

"So . . ." said Bodley, ignoring him. "We need a casting vote. Someone from this crowd to try the last piece of each burger."

A few hands went up.

"Ah, yes, that person there!" said Bodley, pointing.

A man came forward. He had a moustache and pink glasses without any lenses in them. He wore a green rugby shirt and a yellow puffa jacket and a red fluffy top hat and very long orange shorts.

"Hello there!" said the man. "Great to be back! You

may remember I came and had a burger here a while back!"

Benny and Mina and Jasper – and indeed, Lenny – exchanged glances (which was quite a lot of glancing).

"You had a different voice then!" said Benny.

"And a different body!" said Jasper.

"And face!" said Mina.

"Well . . ." said the man. "We all change with time."

"It was a couple of months ago," said Lenny.

The man thought for a moment. "I've been in an accident?"

"An accident that made you taller?" said Benny.

"And your voice deeper?" said Lenny.

"I don't think this matters, does it?" interrupted Bodley. "Whether or not this man is the man who came here before and enjoyed a burger . . . a juicy, succulent burger – and I, for one, see no reason for him to lie about it – he is still a random person picked out of the audience to be the third judge."

"Yes! That's right!" said the man as he reached the stage. "So, take me to the burgers!"

"I'm pretty sure I know who that is . . ." said Benny.

"Yes, so am I," shouted Lenny from the van. "But not sure what we can do about it . . ."

By now the man had approached René von Rathsack's Gourmet Bonkers Big One. The plate was held up for him. He gently moved his moustache – in a way that moustaches are not meant to move – out of the way. Then, just before he bit into the burger, his stomach made a strange noise.

"Oh . . ." he said.

"Do get on with eating the burger, sir," said Bodley.

"Yes. I will." He opened his mouth again. His stomach made the noise again. "Oh no," he muttered.

"What?" said Bodley.

"I think I may just have to . . . Is there a lavatory

nearby . . . Really I . . . it's rather urgent . . ."

"What? Again?"

"I think the smell of the burger may have triggered something in my tummy . . . some gut memory of the –" the man's face went weirdly white – "Laxoform."

"Oh, for heaven's sake . . ." said Bodley. "You can't possibly still be suffering from—"

But the man had gone. He had run away, and in the distance he could be heard saying, "Sorry, can I just nip in and use the . . . No, I don't mind buying a drink. Just let me . . . Oh my God, please!"

Bodley leaned over to Sarah Sherbet and hissed. "Why did he actually *take* Laxoform in the first place? Why couldn't he just *pretend* to have . . ."

"Nick's always been very committed, Bodley," she said. "That's his way of working."

"I see. Well, he's never working for me again. Can I make that clear?"

"Yes, Bodley," said Sarah. "Sorry."

"And you can call me sir from now on," muttered Bodley.

"Hmm . . ." said Lenny. "So, what are we going to do for the casting vote – for the third judge?"

There was a pause. And then:

"Shall I do it?" said a voice from the crowd.

Everyone looked round. A woman made her way through the crowd towards the stage: a very beautiful woman, with long dark hair and a very nice face and a lovely smile. She had her hand up, as if not certain that she would be chosen.

The crowd gasped. Bodley Bonkers stared. Lenny shook his head in disbelief. René von Rathsack frowned. But it was Benny who said with great excitement:

"Juliana Skeffington!"

CHAPTER 38

The crowd broke out into enthusiastic applause. Benny ran out of the van to greet Juliana Skeffington.

"What are you doing here?" he said, his voice full of awe

"Are you Benny?" said Juliana.

"I am."

"Well, I think you called for me," said Juliana. "Didn't you?"

Benny shook his head in wonder. He didn't know what to say.

"Hold on a minute," said Bodley. "It's very good of you to come to the Bracket Wood Bonkers Fry-Off sponsored by **Bonkers Burgers!**, Miss . . . Mrs . . ."

"Ms."

"Right. Ms Juliana."

"Skeffington," said Juliana, looking Bodley directly in the eye.

"Oh. OK, Ms Skeffington. But there is a problem, I'm afraid, if you've come because of Benny."

Juliana raised an eyebrow. "Is there?"

"Well, yes. Because he's one of the chefs, isn't he?" Bodley blustered. "So you might be biased."

"I see," said Juliana, nodding slowly. "You mean . . . unlike the person you choose first of all? Who I saw running into a pub on my way here. Name of Nick Norbert, I believe?"

"Nick . . . who?" said Bodley.

"You know who Nick Norbert is?" said Benny, staring at Juliana.

"I've been following your story quite closely, Benny." She turned back to Bodley, and raised her voice, also addressing the crowd. "Mr Bonkers, I am, as Benny noted, Juliana Skeffington. I have made my name by cooking in an honest and real way. If you are genuinely suggesting that I would taste something in a fry-off . . ."

"The Bracket Wood Bonkers Fry-Off, sponsored by Big Bonkers!" said Bodley.

"Yes. Or any other," Juliana continued. "If you think that I would taste something in a food competition and not completely give my honest opinion as a judge . . . well, I may have to put you in touch with my lawyers."

Bodley thought for a moment. "You don't mean that in a good way, do you?"

"I do not," she answered.

"BOOO! BOOO!" cried the crowd. "BOOO FOR BODLEY!"

And then: "JULIANA! JULIANA! JULIANA!"[17]

Bodley still looked uncertain. Then from behind him René said: "Of coursh I am fine with Msh Shkeffington." He walked round to the front of his cooking station and said: "I know as one great chef to another that she will appreciate only the greatesht food." Then he held his arms out for

17 Which is quite an odd name to chant for a football crowd, but it worked better than you might think.

a hug, saying, "Hi, Julshe."

"Thank you, René," said Juliana, smiling at him. However, she chose not to go in for the hug . . . which left René standing there awkwardly with his arms out.

"OK, OK," said Bodley. "Of course, I trust you, Ms Skeffington. I was only joking. HA HA HA HA HA."

"Right," she said. "Good. Let's taste these burgers!"

CHAPTER 39

It was René's turn first. Juliana went over to his cooking station.

"Sho," said René, as he held up the last section of burger, "I think, given that you will understand in a way that mosht ordinary folksh would not, I should talk you through what I have done here. We sourced a unique piece of wagyu shteak, from one of our own cowsh who are only fed wine, organic mushrooms and mushy peash, and we marinaded the meat for forty-five daysh in a mixsh of olive oil, buttermilk, lemon juice, pot-pourri, more mushy peash, and Gentleman'sh Relish, then we minsh it using my family's own ancient axe from the north of—"

"OK, thanks," said Juliana, picking up the piece of burger and popping it in her mouth.

"Oh," said René. "I had fifteen minutesh more of that shtory to tell."

"Mm-mm," she said, munching away. "Got the gist." She swallowed. "OK. I won't say anything about that for now."

"You won't?" said Bodley.

"No. I'll eat both burgers before I give my opinion," Juliana said matter-of-factly.

Then she glided over to **Lenny's Burgers**. Benny had gone back into the van and was standing on his chair at the grill.

"Hello, Benny."

"Hello, Juliana," said Benny, unable to believe he

was actually speaking to her. He held out the plate with the remaining third of burger.

"Lovely to be here," she said, reaching for it.

"Hey!" said Bodley. "I had to call you Ms Skeffington!"

Ignoring him, she bit into the burger and began, thoughtfully, to chew. Benny searched her face, looking for something – a shutting of the eyes, a small smile maybe, a hint of joy – but she gave nothing away.

She swallowed, and said, "Do you want, like René, to tell me about this burger?"

"Oh . . ." said Benny. He thought for a moment. "No," he said at last.

"Excellent." Juliana turned back to the crowd. "OK! Can both chefs come forward? It's time for the casting vote!"

René and Benny came round from their cooking stations and stood on either side of Juliana.

"So . . ." she began.

"Um, Ms Skeffington?" said Shazad Smith. "Could you announce the winner on the stage? We had it built specially."

Juliana looked round. "Think I'm fine doing it here."

"Oh. OK." And Shazad Smith scuttled away.

"So," said Juliana clearly, "René von Rathsack, your burger was fantastic. It was cooked with tremendous skill. It had an astonishing complexity of flavour, and pushed into a new dimension the very idea of what a burger can be. As soon as I tasted it, I thought, Well, this is impossible to beat."

"Thank you," said René. "Well, shorry, Benny. I guessh you gave it a try . . ."

"There we are!" said Bodley. "What a competition that was! But now, Benny, it's time for you to hand over that cookbook with that secret ingredient and—"

"Hold on," said Juliana sternly. "I haven't finished."

CHAPTER 40

"In many ways, Benny," Juliana said, turning to face him, "your burger wasn't as good. Technically. It didn't taste like something made by a highly trained gourmet chef."

Benny nodded and tried to smile, but he cast his eyes down to the ground.

"Yesh, well, sometimesh the truth hurtsh," said René. Bodley Bonkers, next to him, nodded sadly. But not that sadly.

Juliana ignored them and continued to look at Benny. She crouched down, to his eye level. "But there was something about yours . . . some quality I can't quite name. In the taste."

Benny slowly looked up.

She smiled at him, giving him that wide, generous smile. "It had . . . heart. It moved me. Eating your burger made me feel warm and happy and comforted. It was like a great big hug."

"Oh," said Benny. "Thank you."

Juliana straightened up and faced the crowd.

"Excushe me," said René coldly. "Are you suggeshting that my burger didn't have heart? That it washn't like a great big hug?"

"Well," she said. "You do the maths."

"No, I have a potato chef to do the mash."

"Maths, René."

"Anyway it doesh have heart in it. Cow heart."

"That's awful," said Mina.

"Offal, yes," said Bodley.

"Anyway!" said Juliana. "At the moment, to be honest, it's a draw."

The crowd let out a collective sigh of frustration. They'd been waiting for a while now and they wanted a winner.

"But . . ." Juliana raised a hand to quieten the impatient audience. "I need to ask one question that may help me work out a winner."

She turned to René von Rathsack. "René, I've heard a lot from you about your meat . . . where it came from, how expensive it was, and so on."

"Oh, yesh. But there wash fifteen minutshe more, as I shaid, and what I didn't tell you was that—"

"No, I don't need to know any more," Juliana said firmly. She turned to the **Lenny's Burgers** van. "What I do need to know though, Benny, is . . . where did you get your meat for your burger?"

"Oh," said Benny. "Um . . ." His eyes flicked to Mina, who was standing in front of the van. She met his gaze and did a little fist pump . . . which meant: go for it.

"Local organic butcher's? Farmers' market?" Juliana offered. "A supermarket, perhaps?"

Benny cleared his throat and spoke at last: "It's . . . uh . . . a vegan burger."

There was an audible gasp from the crowd. The word "vegan" was being whispered a lot, along with

"Not meat?" and "I can't believe it!" and "Eh?"

Juliana frowned. "Vegan?"

"Yes," said Benny. "My friend Mina got the vegan mince. That's what I used to make the basic patty."

Mina waved a nervous hand at Juliana.

"But then," Benny went on, "to make it more meat-like, I added some garlic and herbs and seasoning . . . and kneaded it by hand . . . and . . . stuff."

Juliana looked stunned.

Meanwhile, René walked over to Benny. "You went up againsht me – René von Rathsack – with a . . . a vegan burger?"

Benny nodded.

"Pah!" uttered René, turning away. "What kind of competition ish this?"

"Well," said Bodley to Juliana, "I think that's that, isn't it? I mean, really. It seems clear to me just from that information alone who the winner should be."

Juliana took a long look at him, and then nodded. She turned to the crowd.

"You're correct, Bodley. I declare the winner of this fry-off—"

"The Bracket Wood Bonkers Fry-off, sponsored by **Bonkers Burgers!**" said Bodley Bonkers, running over to René, to stand by him for the special moment of announcement.

"The winner is," Juliana declared, "Benny!"

CHAPTER 41

The crowd roared as Juliana went over to Benny and raised his arm, a bit like a referee does in a boxing match.

"What?" said Bodley Bonkers.

"What?" said René von Rathsack.

"What?" said Shazad Smith.

"What?" said . . . Oh, you get the point.

Everyone said, "What?" Including Benny.

"Yes," said Juliana.

"But I thought I'd lost," said Benny. "Because I cooked a vegan burger."

"No, Benny," said Juliana, loud enough for the crowd to hear. "If I may be honest with you, I felt embarrassed. I'm a professional chef. I like to think I'm quite a good one, and that I have a very good palate."

"Pilot?"

"Palate. Mouth, basically. What I'm saying is that I think of myself as someone with pretty sensitive taste buds."

"We love you, Juliana!" shouted someone in the crowd.

"Yes, well. Thank you. But I failed. As a taster. Because you had made your burger so well. It was a draw, but this is what pushed it over the line: the fact that your burger was so good that I couldn't even tell it was a vegan one. Point being, you cooked it so well it doesn't matter whether it was meat or not – it was just a really good burger!"

The crowd cheered again, apart from perhaps three people who were still shaking their heads and saying, "Not meat?"

René von Rathsack approached Benny. He was putting a coat on – and seemed to be having difficulty

"OK. Enough already. I am returning to Smørgöswispa – where, by the way, I have won . . ." He heaved the coat on at last. There was a jangling sound. On the front of the coat were a lot of tiny toilets. Well, not actual working toilets. Who would they be for? Hamsters? No. Tiny models. Of toilets. "Eighteen Sanitaire medals!"

Juliana frowned. "You wear them on your coat? All the time?"

"I thought you said you didn't make a fuss?" said Bodley Bonkers.

"There's only seventeen," said Jasper.

"The new one hasn't been sent yet!" shouted René, walking off. "Also my tailor saysh that if I put another one on this coat it might tear! It's already mush too heavy . . ."

And he was gone.

"Amazing that they are actually tiny toilets . . ." said Lenny.

CHAPTER 42

"Well . . ." said Bodley Bonkers. "That's that, then. I suppose."

"I don't think so," said Juliana. "There's a small matter, I believe, of a bet . . ."

"Oh, yes." Bodley turned to Milly Mackay. "Surely our lawyers can sort this one?" he said.

Milly shrugged and shook her head. "I think it's on camera, sir. You making the bet, I mean."

Bodley looked furious. "I've had enough of this.

Michael! Michaela! Just take the cookbook! Don't let anyone stand in your way!"

Michael looked at Michaela. Michaela looked at Michael.

"Can't do that."

"I beg your pardon, Michael."

"I'm Michaela."

"Oh, um, I beg your pardon, Michaela . . ."

"Can't do that," said Michaela. "A bet's a bet."

"A promise is a promise," said Michael.

Bodley's face turned rather red. "What? But I'm your boss!"

"Yeah. But some things . . ." said Michael.

"Are bigger than that," said Michaela.

"Oh, for heaven's sake!" exclaimed Bodley. He went over to Benny and Lenny. "OK, OK. You can have it! The Bracket Wood store! I have forty-five others anyway! And that one was becoming a pain. You're welcome to it!"

Benny and Lenny didn't quite know what to say to this. But someone else had something to say:

"Uh. . . sir?"

"Yes?" said Bodley.

It was Margot, the server at **Bonkers Burgers!** She was wearing her uniform.

"Um. . . what does that mean for me? And the rest of the staff?"

She looked around, and four other people in **Bonkers Burgers!** uniforms came forward, all looking troubled.

Bodley shrugged. "Dunno. You'll have to ask your new bosses."

"Well . . . no," said Margot. "You're still our boss. We're all under contract to **Bonkers Burgers!** We're not allowed to work for anyone else."

Bodley thought about this for a minute. Then he shrugged again. "Not my problem any more."

Margot looked crestfallen. She turned her gaze

to Benny and Lenny.

"Dad?" said Benny. "What shall we do?"

"Um . . ." said Lenny quietly. "Thing is, Small Fry . . . it might be for the best."

Benny frowned. "What might be?"

"Not taking the restaurant back." Lenny sighed. "I mean . . . I was angry about it for years. And when you made the bet I wanted us to win it back. But now . . . I think going back there now . . . might not be good for me. That was in the past. And I think – I hope – I've moved on." He glanced at his van and patted it. "And, also, I've kind of grown to love this old thing."

Benny nodded. "That's OK, Dad," he said. "That opens up a new possibility."

CHAPTER 43

Benny turned to Bodley Bonkers, who was sitting glumly on the edge of the stage.

"Er . . . Mr Bonkers?"

"Oh, for heaven's sake. My real name is Jeremy. Jeremy Pickle."

"Is it?"

"Yes."

"Hello, Mr Pickle." Benny paused. "Actually, I think that would have been quite a good name for the head of a burger company . . ."

"Yes. Maybe. It's probably a bit late in the day though for me to change it back again."

"Yes, I agree," said Benny. "Let's stick with Bodley Bonkers. So, Mr Bonkers, about our bet . . . I have a different deal to offer you."

Bodley sighed. "Right, well, just put it in writing and then send it to Shazad Smith. Or Milly Mackay. Or Sally Sherbet. I mean, whoever. Who knows what they all do?"

"Can't I just tell you my idea now?" asked Benny.

Bodley frowned. "Oh, I suppose so."

Benny took a deep breath. "So, the Bracket Wood City Farm."

"What about it?"

"It was sold recently. To **Bonkers Burgers!**"

Bodley looked at his team. "Which one of you can tell me if this is right?"

Shazad Smith gingerly put his hand up. "Um, yes.

Benny is correct. We bought it. To redevelop the land and put a new store there."

"Right." Bodley turned back to Benny. "And?"

"And I want you to leave it as a farm."

Bodley's frown deepened.

Mina rushed over from the front of the van. "Oh, Benny! That's so great! How fantastic! Dottie and all the others can stay there! And they won't be—"

"Hang on," said Bodley. "Shazad, how much will this cost us? Keeping it as a farm."

Shazad thought for a moment. He counted a sum on his fingers and then leaned over to whisper to Bodley.

"A farm, by the way," said Benny, "where you don't slaughter any animals for beef burgers."

Shazad stopped whispering and stood up straight. He did the sum again on his fingers. Then he leaned in again and whispered to Bodley.

"What? Really?" Bodley exclaimed.

Shazad nodded.

Bodley looked at Benny. "That's not going to be possible," he said.

Benny stared back at him. Then he looked to Mina, who screwed up her face.

"What are we going to do?" she said.

Benny took another deep breath.

"What if I offer you my grandad's cookbook? With the secret ingredient?"

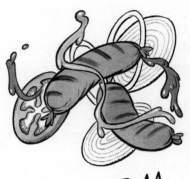

CHAPTER 44

Bodley considered Benny's offer. "Really? No tricks? No mucking about? It'll really be the whole cookbook, with the secret ingredient?"

"Yes," said Benny, nodding.

"Benny . . ." said Mina. "Are you sure about this?"

"Yes," added Juliana. "A chef ought to be careful about giving up their secrets . . ."

"I'm sure," said Benny.

Bodley peered at him, his eyes squinting. He

looked for a long time. In fact, he brought his face a little too close to Benny's for Benny's liking. Benny wanted to back away, but in the end just stayed there, standing his ground, not blinking.

"It's a deal," said Bodley eventually, finally stepping back.

"Right!" said Benny. He went to the van and stepped inside.

And didn't come out. For quite a while.

In fact, it became a bit awkward outside the van. The crowd began talking among themselves. Bodley and Juliana both stood there waiting, while René von Rathsack's team began dismantling his outdoor cooking station.

"Um . . . you didn't like the name Pickle?" Juliana said to Bodley.

"No," he replied. "Boys at school called me Sour."

"Not Sweet 'n' Sour?"

He looked at her. "No."

"OK," said Juliana.

"Here it is!" said Benny at last, emerging from the van. He smoothed his hand over the cover, dusting it off before holding it up. "Kenny's Cookbook!"

Bodley welcomed the news with open arms, as Benny came over to him and Juliana.

"OK! Shazad! Milly! Sarah!" They all stepped forward and stood by Bodley. "I'd like you all to witness this. Once I take this book, it is the property of **Bonkers Burgers!** And the recipe for the burger, with the secret ingredient, will belong only to Bonkers and Co. Inc. LLP Ltd . . .!"

"What do those letters mean?" said Benny.

"I don't know!" said Bodley. "But what I do know," he said, stretching out a hand, "is that the cookbook is now mine."

"Hang on!" said Benny, holding it out of Bodley's reach. "Dad! Mina! Jasper! And, um, Juliana?"

They all came forward and stood by Benny, who

said, "I want you to witness that once I hand this over, that Bonkers and Co. Inc., er, L . . . L . . ."

"P," offered Bodley.

"P. Then what?"

"Limited."

"OK. All that," said Benny. "So, I want everyone to witness that you and your company promise to keep Bracket Wood City Farm as a farm, with the animals . . . um . . . alive."

Bodley nodded impatiently. "Yes."

"Promise?"

"Yes, yes. I promise. Now give me that book!"

And so Benny handed it over.

"Right, right, right!" Bodley said eagerly, flicking through the pages and reading bits out loud. "Let's see . . . Sausage sandwich – don't care much about that . . . Brown sauce, really? I prefer red . . . Anyway . . . Beans on toast – is there really any need for a recipe for that? Hmm, cheese toasties – yes, best with cheddar, I agree . . . Ah! Here we go. Beef burger!"

His eyes scanned the page. Once. Twice.

"Beef patty . . . lettuce, tomato . . . burger sauce, made with ketchup and mayo . . . and a bun." He looked up and laughed "HA HA HA HA!" but not in a good way.

"Sorry. Have I missed something?"

"No," said Benny.

"Well, excuse me, but none of those are the secret ingredients of a burger."

"The secret ingredient – for all of Kenny's recipes, not just burgers – is at the start of the book," Benny said calmly. "You missed it."

"I did?"

"Yes. It's on the first page."

"Sorry," said Bodley, flicking to the front of the book. "I saw the first page . . . It's just a picture of –" he held the page up for all to see – "some smiling young woman."

Benny nodded. "That's my mum," he said.

CHAPTER 45

Bodley frowned. "Right. Um. Great. Whatevs."

"Her name was Rose," continued Benny. "That's her when she was young. A bit older than I am now."

"OK. But excuse me – how the blazes is that a secret recipe, if you please?"

"Well . . ." said Benny, glancing at Lenny, who was looking on intently, "I never really knew my mum. She died when I was young. But my dad tells me she was lovely . . ."

"She was," said Lenny softly.

"And Kenny, of course, was her dad," said Benny. "So, if you look at what he wrote underneath . . ."

Bodley scanned the page again. "To Rose – these dishes were all made with her in mind." He looked up. "Sorry, I still don't get it."

Benny blinked. "What it means, Mr Bonkers, is that all these dishes were made with love. And that is the secret ingredient: love. Always make food like you're making it for someone you love. Because as Juliana always says . . ." he said, turning to her.

"Cooking isn't just about food – it's about love!" said Juliana joyfully.

Bodley stared at her. Then at Benny.

"Right. So that's it, is it? The secret ingredient. Love. Really?"

"Yes," said Benny.

"Of course!" said Juliana, beaming. "That was what I was tasting! In Benny's burger! When I said it had heart – I get it now! That's why it felt like a great big hug."

Bodley snorted. He threw **Kenny's Cookbook** to the ground.

"That's rubbish!" he shouted. "You know what an

ingredient is? Salt. Pepper. Onions. Cheese."

"Spoons," said Shazad Smith.

"No, not spoons. That's cutlery."

"Oh, sorry."

"Flour. Tomatoes. Curry powder. Milk," continued Bodley. "Not this hokey sentimental nonsense. Love is not an ingredient!"

"Isn't it?" said Lenny, coming forward. Delicately, he picked up the cookbook and dusted it off. "Well, I saw you when you came to my van in disguise, pretending to be someone else, so you could try Benny's burger. I watched you when you had your first bite. You shut your eyes. You could hardly move. What did you feel, Mr Bonkers? What made you like that?"

Bodley looked uncomfortable. He stared at his feet. "Well . . . yes, I admit it was nice . . ."

"Nice doesn't cover it. You were dumbstruck by the taste."

"Well . . . OK. It made me feel . . . I suppose it made me feel . . ."

"What?" said Juliana softly. "What did it make you feel, Bodley?"

She reached out and took his hand. He looked up at her smiling, caring face.

"LOVED!" shouted Bodley. "YES! ALL RIGHT! YES! IT MADE ME FEEL LOVED!"

"Yes . . ." said Juliana.

"LIKE THE PERSON WHO MADE THE BURGER FOR ME WAS MY MUMMY! ONLY NOT MY ACTUAL MUMMY! BECAUSE SHE DIDN'T LOVE ME! OR AT LEAST NEVER SHOWED IT! SHE WAS ALWAYS CROSS AND MADE ME WEAR A BOW TIE WHEN I WAS FIVE . . . AND AT SCHOOL EVERYONE CALLED ME BOW-TIE BUM-BUM!"

"OK," said Juliana. "Maybe we don't need to know *everything* about how you fel—"

"AND SHE NEVER MADE ME FOOD LIKE THAT

BURGER. THAT BURGER TASTED LIKE MY DREAM MUMMY HAD MADE IT! THE MUMMY I ALWAYS WANTED!"

And with that, he burst into tears and fell into Juliana's arms. A tiny bit embarrassed, she patted Bodley Bonkers back, saying, "Um, there, there. There, now."

Everyone else looked at each other, not knowing what to say.

Eventually Benny spoke up:

"Well, I guess it is a real secret ingredient then."

CHAPTER 46

"I can't believe they kept their word," said Mina, looking out over Bracket Wood City Farm.

It was a few days later, and the deadline for the sale of the farm had come and gone.

"Yes," said Benny. They were leaning on the fence that separated them from the main field. "I guess so. I mean, all the animals are still here."

"Yes," said Mina, smiling. Then, she added, blushing, "I'd like them to know."

Benny frowned. "Who?"

"The animals. I'd sort of like them to know what we – well, mainly what you did for them."

Benny laughed. "What we both did, Mina." He looked at the field. "Not that it matters. They'll just keep on munching the grass . . ."

As he said this though, Dottie the cow looked up, as if she recognised the sound of his voice. She was indeed munching some grass. But then she came over slowly – cows generally don't move quickly – looking at him unblinkingly the whole time.

"Hello, Dottie!" said Mina. "Did you know we were talking about you?"

Dottie licked her lips.

"Have you come over to say thank you to Benny?"

Mina looked to Benny, gesturing with her hand. It was enough to make Dottie turn her enormous head and look at him. And it was probably just a fly . . . but something made her bob that enormous head

up and down, once up and once down, as if to say,
"Yes. I have."

Which made Mina and Benny laugh with joy – a
lot – until a voice from behind them said:

"Oy! What are you two doing? It's work time!"

CHAPTER 47

The voice was Lenny's, who had driven to the farm to pick them up and take them back to the van, parked and waiting, as ever, outside The Bracket.

"Did you forget it was Saturday?" he said, as they stepped through the side door of **Lenny's Burgers**. Jasper was there already, waiting to start. "And that we are all meant to be here at least half an hour before I open the van to customers?"

"Sorry, Dad," said Benny. "We were just having a great time with the animals!"

"OK, well . . . get those vegan patties out." Lenny grinned. "You may have fooled Juliana Skeffington into thinking that was a beef burger, but today you're going to have to do it again and again, my boy. With –" he began opening the shutters – "the people who really count!"

Light flooded into the van, blinding Benny for a second. When he could see properly, blinking, he looked out.

And saw the longest queue ever! It seemed to go on and on, all round The Bracket and probably round again.

At the front was Edith, who was waving a local paper.

"Hey, Benny! Look!" she shouted.

She held up the paper. The front page said:

L BOY BEATS BEST CHEF IN THE WORLD

URGER OFF!

L WINS!

Rene von
thsack
feated!

e chef known simply as
Fry" has defeated world
chef René von Rathsack
inkers Burgers sponsored
Off event this past week. The
is were competing for title of-

Many spectators say that the cooking
smells coming from Small Fry's small
grill were amazing.
"I didn't get to taste it, but I know
it had to be insanely good. Smelled
waaay better than the stuff that the
famous chef guy was cooking up,"
said one local football club fan.
"Oh, I've been buying burgers from
Small Fry and his dad for a while
now. Gotta say they are the best
burgers I've ever eaten. I'm not
surprised at all that he won that-

"Wow!" said Benny.

"Yes," said Jasper. "I'm surprised they didn't say 'fry-off'."

"Burger, please!" shouted someone.

"And for me!"

"Two for me!"

"With onions!"

"I'll have one," called a familiar voice from somewhere behind Edith. "And make sure you put in loads of the special ingredient!"

Mina gasped: "Juliana Skeffington! In the queue!"

"OMG," said Benny. "Shouldn't you . . . you know . . . jump to the front? VIP treatment and all that?"

"Oh no," said Juliana. "Happy to wait. I've become a bit of a Bracket Wood FC fan!" she said, holding up a blue scarf.

"Goodness."

"Come on, Small Fry, get the grill on!" shouted Edith.

Benny smiled.

"You know what, Benny?" said Lenny. "I like calling you that. But I think, after all you've done . . . Yes, I reckon I'm going to call you something else from now on."

"What?" said Benny.

Lenny grinned. "Having a think about it."

"OK," said Benny, tying up his chef's whites. He got up on his stool at the cooking area, then announced loudly: "Mina: get the salad going. Jasper: sauce. And Dad: turn on the grill."

"You got it, Chef," said Lenny, smiling.

Acknowledgements

Thanks in the creation of this book must go to my fantastic illustrator Cory Loftis; to my agent, Georgia Garrett; all at HarperCollins Children's Books, especially Tom Bonnick, Nick Lake, Cally Poplak, Matt Kelly, Elorine Grant, Jane Baldock, Sam White, and Jess Williams; Tanya Hougham and Patch for the audiobook; and once again, Ezra Banks-Baddiel for giving me the basic idea (after we went to a drive-in McDonalds and he said, "what if some young guy who worked here was actually a brilliant chef?").